SLIDER

STACY BOREL

Slider

Stacy Borel

Copyright © 2015

Cover Design by Kari from Cover to Cover

Editing by Missy Borucki

Interior Design by Formatting by KassiCoop

SLIDER

PROLOGUE

Annabelle

THE SUN SHONE BRIGHT in Athens, Georgia. I was spending the afternoon with my friend, Keegan at her boyfriend's parent's house. We'd just did the grand "march across the stage to be handed a blank piece of paper that was supposed to represent our diploma" ceremony. Graduating from nursing school had been a big deal, but my day was severely dampened by the fact that my parents were not in attendance. I didn't necessarily feel alone, or like each step I took across the stage would cause me to suddenly burst into tears because nobody was here to cheer me on in the crowd. It felt more like a simmering anger down in my gut that, once again, this was a milestone I was celebrating on my own. When you've been an orphan since the ripe old age of sixteen, you not only start to accept the quiet, you welcome it. You learn to hold your shoulders back instead of slouched from defeat. You become strong in the moments of weakness and I've become my own support system. On this day though, I felt like a cloud was hovering over my moment of joviality. I wanted to see my mother's bright red hair blowing in the wind, smiling as she held a Kleenex to her reddened eyes. I wanted to see my father clapping and cheering me on as if this day belonged to only me. Instead, they weren't here, and every fiber of my being felt saturated in sadness. I switched that emotion to anger because it felt more tangible. So when Keegan asked me to come spend time with the Brooks family, I accepted. I wanted to feel a connection, even if it wasn't my own. I wanted to surround myself with a family. I was appreciative of her offer, that is until it wound up being a giant pain in my ass . . . or ankle as it happened.

The Brooks family had a tradition that they played baseball every time they got together. This family took their baseball seriously, as evidenced by their boys being named after baseball stadiums. Keegan really wanted me to hang out after lunch to play. I wasn't so sure I should have for a couple of reasons: one, I wasn't really wearing appropriate clothing for outdoor activities, and two, I had never played baseball before in my life. However, hearing her excitement for the game is what changed my mind. It was fun watching the family pick teams, and heckling one another about who was going to win. Family dynamics always gave me a twinge of something. I wouldn't call it jealousy, because that wasn't the right word. No, it was more like envy. Their family unit was something I desired in my own life. Yeah, I was envious of their connection.

As the game progressed, all was going well until it was my turn to bat. I hit a grounder and began running the bases. I rounded third but, unfortunately, my foot caught the lip of the base and down I went, *hard*. There I lay, splayed out in the dirt, and my pride sitting somewhere back at second base. Pain shot through my ankle the moment I tried to lift myself from the ground to stand. Wincing, I grabbed my leg, cursing under my breath. Son of a bitch, that hurt! Looks like fashion didn't beat out practical today. I heard the sound of shoes crunching on the ground coming up beside me. Somehow, I instinctively knew who it was before his shadow shrouded over me blocking the sun. My eyes ran the length of him. Up and up I glanced, taking in every inch that was Turner Brooks. I noted just how tall he really was. From this angle, he was a giant. Then again, my butt was currently on the ground in a non-graceful manner so, of course, he looked ginormous. My tummy did a little flip when I made eye contact with his crystal blue ones. He took a moment to look me over, probably deciphering what kind of idiot I really was, before he crouched down beside me.

"You alright?" he asked.

The deep baritone of his voice made my breath catch. I simply nodded. Keegan came running up to my other side and I turned my gaze in her direction. Her face was etched with concern. I really hated the look of pity she was giving me. Don't feel sorry for me. Don't *ever* feel sorry for me.

"Annabelle, can you roll it this way?" Turner asked, bringing my attention back to him.

I tried to wiggle my now tender ankle. The moment I moved it, pain sliced through my foot and I hissed. Could this day get any crazier? I shook my head. "How embarrassing! I'm so sorry for ruining the game." I placed my face in my palms.

"Hush," Turner scolded. I glanced up at him, taken aback by his tone. "You didn't ruin anything. Accidents happen all the time, plus you're wearing flip flops, so that didn't help."

I was about to say something when Keegan jumped in and spoke. "Turner, scolding her isn't helping anyone." Keegan may be smal, but the glare she gave him was fierce. "Can you at least tell if it's broken?"

I peered between the two of them and watched a silent show down take place. Turner's jaw was clenched in frustration. I couldn't tell if it was toward Keegan or me, but I could only assume it was the latter. Of course he was frustrated with me, we were all having fun and I interrupted it because I so gracefully decided to see what the dirt tasted like. *Awesome.* Keegan, on the other hand, just looked confused. Turner reached out and gingerly lifted my foot, supporting it with one hand under my heel, while his other hand tenderly pressed around my ankle.

"Doesn't feel like anything's broken, but you're going to have to sit out the rest of the game." I was disappointed because I was enjoying myself. *Wonderful first impression, Annabelle.* I silently told myself. "In fact, I think you need to go back to the house and get some ice on it before it starts swelling," Turner stated.

As a new RN, you would think that I would have thought about the ice . . . nope! I looked at Keegan. "I can't believe this happened, I'm not normally this clumsy." Except I really am. I could trip and fall even while standing completely still.

The confused look Keegan held earlier was now wiped away. Her blue eyes were soft when she replied, "No worries. I just hope that you're okay." She turned towards her boyfriend, Camden, whom is probably the second hottest guy I'd ever seen, (we don't need to talk about the man currently hovering over me taking first place in that category) and asked if he could come help me get on the golf cart. Just as Camden started walking towards me, two strong arms lifted me in the air and I instinctively wrapped my arms around Turner's neck.

"I've got her," he replied as he moved us away from everyone. I had no doubt they were all looking on in confusion.

"What are you doing? I could have walked you know."

He rolled his eyes. "No, you couldn't. You already tried to wiggle it and look how far that got you. Just hush and let me get you on the cart."

The little butterflies in my tummy were fluttering wildly now. Turner was currently caring for me as if he knew what he was doing. I was aware that Camden owned a gym, so I imagine they all knew what to do in case someone got injured. But I felt like I was a hindrance to his game with his family. Getting a headache right between my eyes, I closed my mouth and chose not to argue, and just relax until we got back to the house. When Turner set me on the overheated plastic seat, he didn't give me a second glance as he rounded the front and slid in next to me. Turning back towards the field, I noticed the game had resumed but Keegan stopped and gave me a small wave and a sad smile. I lifted my hand in return just before Turner drove us away. Every little bump on the road jarred my ankle and I gritted my teeth to keep from whining about the pace he was driving. Surely he must know the jostling was making the injury ache. Clenching my fists in the seat, I saw Turner glance down at my hands and he let off of the gas a little, but he remained quiet. I thought he might've asked if I was doing alright, but he didn't. He stayed quiet just as I was. Folding my arms over my chest, I closed my eyes and let the steady hum of the engine relax me until I felt us coming to a stop.

As Turner shut off the cart, I opened my eyes and swung my legs out and used the back of the seat to lift myself up while I held my sore leg up. He came around to me and acted as if he were going to pick me up again. This time I held my hand up to stop him.

Shaking my head I said, "No, I've got it."

"Annabelle, I can easily carry you inside."

I met his blue eyes. "I said, *no*." His jaw ticked and he huffed before we walked into the house.

I gave a little hop, letting go of the seat. Wobbling, I almost lost my balance but regained control and hopped again. I made a few more jumps, grabbing on to things in the garage as I went along. A very frustrated looking Turner stood at the door to the mud room. When I finally made it to him, he looked down at me. He was already much taller than my five-foot-five stature, but when he was standing up on the step, he towered over me. As if trying to intimidate me with his size, he continued to block the entrance into the house. My leg that was currently holding all of my weight was getting tired and I desperately just wanted to sit down. Grasping the door frame I gave a little jump and nearly bumped into him when I hopped inside. He stepped back before our bodies touched and admittedly I was slightly disappointed that he did. Shaking it off, I looked at him over my shoulder, hobbling my way through the narrow hall.

"Can you show me where a rag is for the ice? I'm not comfortable digging around your mother's kitchen." I turned and started making my way ahead of him.

I heard Turner grumble before he responded with, "Yeah, I'll get one."

I noticed the food from lunch was still on the counters and I looked around the spacious room. Walnut colored cabinets lined a U-shaped kitchen set with a beautiful golden hued granite, and stainless steel appliances. There was an island in the middle that had a small rooster pitcher as a decoration. I reached towards it to help balance myself while Turner went to get a cloth. Everything about this place screamed country chic and warmth. If I ever moved out of my parent's house or redecorated it on my own, this is what I'd want. The room made you feel welcome, like you wanted to sit down and eat a slice of pie and have a cup of coffee. I looked up when Turner came back in the kitchen and headed toward the freezer to gather some ice cubes. I swallowed, feeling the little butterflies making another appearance. Why did he make me feel this way?

When we had been eating lunch I watched him, my eyes intermittently wandered to where he'd been sitting. I didn't *want* to look at him, but I felt a pull to. I was curious about him. He was no doubt the best good looking man I think I'd ever seen. I watched him with prying eyes as he had spoken to his dad. He was calm—relaxed, but there was an undertone of unease. His blue eyes held a wealth of knowledge and the words that rolled off his tongue were that of an educated man. Turner held his shoulders high and his back straight. I'd never seen shoulders so broad. But then

SLIDER

again, as I glanced around the table, every male in this family had the same stature. Turner came across as dominant, those waves that traveled off of him quiet and strong. It was as though little invisible crests moved through the room and wrapped around you, silently pulling you in without you even knowing it. It was unnerving.

Taking another look at him while he moved through the kitchen, I drank in his good looks. He had high cheek bones and a strong square jaw sporting a five o'clock shadow. My fingers tips tingled in an odd way to reach up and brush them across the rough surface. The urge to graze a man's skin was never something that I ever really battled with. And it wasn't because I had never *wanted* to touch a man, it was that I stuffed down the desires like an unwanted annoyance. I realized I was attracted to him.

Not good.

As Turner came toward me, I did what I always do . . . remained indifferent. I looked up at him when he stood in front of me, meeting his crystal eyes head on. I felt the dominance coming off of him but I shrugged the sensation off and made a small hop towards the breakfast nook. There was a little table with two chairs and I really just wanted to take a moment to rest. Before I was able to get any further, hands came under my arms and Turner lifted me up like a small child and set me on the island. The stone was cool under my legs. I wanted to protest that he had picked me up again without my permission, but the relief of not standing anymore was enough to keep my mouth shut. I saw a small smile quirk at the corner of his full lips, and I wondered if he expected me to say something.

"Lift your leg and rest your ankle on your knee, please."

I raised a brow. "The brute has manners. Interesting."

I did as he asked and he gently placed the rag over my already swollen ankle.

"Of course I have manners. What made you think I didn't?" he asked, confused.

I felt my own mouth fighting off a smile. "It's just that you have picked me up twice now without asking me, and then you didn't even bother apologizing for invading my personal space. So hearing a 'please' come from you is . . . nice."

He grinned. "The doctor in me tends to act before considering that I may be being intrusive. So for that, I apologize."

"Doctor?" I asked inquisitively.

"Keegan never told you?" His piercing blue eyes met mine.

I shook my head. "No. I only know a little about Camden and Dodger. Before today, I hadn't really even remembered Camden had two other brothers."

His boyish grin grew wider and the fluttering in my tummy did a summer sault. "I'm a Fellow at UGA Medical."

This was complete news to me. During lunch he had asked me what field I was interested in working. I answered saying Sports Medicine or Labor and Delivery. He pushed me a little further and asked which one I wanted to be in more. I didn't really know. I favored sports medicine, but when it came to having a job, it didn't really matter. I just wanted to be a nurse and help people. Besides, I couldn't continue to live off of my parent's life insurance and investments. Okay, well, technically I could, but I wanted to have my own money.

Clearing my throat, I reached down to take the icy cloth away from him to hold myself. His eyes followed the direction of my hand before he looked up at me through his lashes. Stepping back and leaning against the opposite counter, he crossed his arms over his broad chest and watched me. Turner made me nervous with his scrutiny, and I squirmed. Feeling incapable of meeting his eyes, I looked down at my leg and picked at nonexistent fuzz on my shorts.

"So, as a fellow, you've already done your residency?" I asked, trying to redirect my thoughts.

When he didn't answer I gave him my eyes. "I have, yes."

The way he was looking at me caused me to blush. Uhhh, I don't blush. "In what department is your fellowship?"

The corner of his mouth twitched. "Sports Medicine."

My eyebrows shot up. "Wait, if I went into Sports Med, we would be working together."

"Yes, we would. Would that be a bad thing?"

I looked back down at my hands. "No. But now I understand why you asked. I just don't think it's a department that will have any openings when I go apply next week."

"I could always put in a good word for you if you'd like."

"No!" I said too loudly, meeting his blue eyes again. "I mean, no, but thank you. I'd like to do this on my own."

He nodded. "Understood." Dropping his arms back down to his sides, he pointed to my leg. "You can take the ice off now."

I glanced down. "Oh, right." I lifted the cloth from my leg and set it on the counter beside me. I was about to thank him for helping me when sounds came from the back door.

"I swear you two are going to end up killing each other," Wrigley said to Dodger as they walked into the kitchen completely oblivious to Turner and me.

"Whatever, little brother. Mind your own damn business," Dodger growled.

Wrigley chuckled and held his hands up in the air. "Hey, man, all I'm saying is, work your shit out. Macie still digs you, but both of you are being stubborn. Just tell her you're sorry and move on."

Dodger grabbed a water bottle from the fridge and tilted his head back as he downed the entire thing. When he finished, he tossed the bottle into the trash and pointed across the kitchen toward Wrigley. "I'm going to say this once, and the next time you bring it up, I swear I'll kick your ass. Leave it, *alone*. Macie and I are not your concern and never will be. Besides, you wouldn't know how a relationship worked if it bit you in the ass."

Wrigley chugged his own bottle of water. "Sure I would. I do relationships all the time."

"Sticking your dick in a girl isn't the equivalent to having a relationship."

Turner was grinning and let out a huff in agreement. I looked up at the mammoth of a man that had moved to stand next to me and wondered what on earth he could be smiling about. In fact, I felt weird being witness to this little sibling argument. Donna, the boy's mother, had taken that moment to walk into the kitchen and gasped.

"Boys, you better not be talking about what I think you're talking about. There are ladies present and that's something your mother just doesn't want to hear."

"No worries, Ma, the conversation is over," Dodger replied.

She turned and glared, pointing a finger at her youngest son, Wrigley. "You, mister, had better be wrapping it up if you are having sex. In fact, just stop it! No more sex until you're married. The last thing I want to find out is that you got some girl pregnant."

"Jesus, Mom! I'm not talking to you about this." Wrigley actually had the sense to appear embarrassed. Turner and Dodger smirked at their little brother's discomfort. "Anyway, change of subject. Hey, Mom, what do you call a guy with no arms or legs in a pile of leaves?"

There was a collective groan in the room. "Wrig, not now," Turner scolded

He ignored them. "Russell." He slapped his leg, laughing at his own joke. I let a giggle slip out. In my defense, it was pretty funny. Turner turned to eye me and tilted his head to the side. I shrugged. "Oh man, Belle, did you just laugh? Holy shit, *finally* someone who appreciates my jokes." Wrigley came over to me and slung his arm around my shoulder.

My face turned redder than my hair and I looked away from everyone. "I hadn't heard that one before. It was kind of funny."

He ruffled my hair like I was a child. What was it about these Brooks boys doing that? "You're cute."

Turner smacked Wrigley's arm off of me and glowered. "First of all, her name is Annabelle, not *Belle* and second, she was just being polite. Keep your hands to yourself, shithead."

"Actually," I spoke to Turner. "Belle is fine, the joke was funny, and thank you for the compliment." I turned to Wrigley and gave a soft smile.

"Ha! In your face, asshole."

"Boys," Donna chastised. Changing the subject, she came over to me and looked at my ankle. "How are you feeling, sweetie? Anything I can get you?"

With all of the commotion going on, I'd completely forgotten about my injury. "No, thank you though. Actually, I think I'm going to get going. It's been a long day and I'm feeling pretty tired."

"Okay, honey. Shall I get one of my boys to drive you home? I'm sure they wouldn't mind."

"No, I appreciate it, but I think I can make on my own—"

"I'll drive her." Turner interrupted me.

I twisted to face him, my red hair whipping around. "It's fine, I said I'll drive myself."

His face became hard as stone, and those dominant waves silently worked their way over to me. "I will drive you home in your car, and Dodger can follow behind us to bring me back here."

I swallowed down the feeling to comply. What on earth was up with this guy? A girl says no, she means it. At least when I said no, I did. "No, thank you." My voice was strong and firm. There was no room for budging and I didn't like his sudden change of demeanor.

SLIDER

Donna piped up, "She's got it, Turner, leave the poor girl be." She leaned in and hugged me. It was the kindest gesture I'd been given in a long time and a lump formed in my throat. "It was so wonderful meeting you. Please, don't be a stranger. You're welcome here anytime. Oh, and congratulations on graduating." Her smile was so sincere and comforting. I wanted to pull her back into a tight embrace just to feel that motherly warmth, and then run back into my cocoon of silence. Instead, I reciprocated her smile and thanked her for her hospitality.

Scooting off the counter, I saw out of the corner of my eye Turner's hands twitch to assist me. He probably would have had his mom not been there to slap him away if he tried. I grabbed my purse that I set on the counter opposite me, and started to hobble my way to the door. A slow burn started up my leg, but I refused to ask for help. I looked over my shoulder and plastered on a polite smile. "It was very nice meeting you all. Thank you again for having me. I'm sorry I was such a bother here at the end."

Just as I reached for the knob, a heavy hand landed on my shoulder. "Seriously, Annabelle, I can drive you home. I don't mind."

I flipped around to face him. "Truly, I appreciate it, but I'd rather drive myself."

"Okay, this is going to seem like it's coming from left field, but I have to ask." He seemed to steel himself for whatever the question would be. He took a deep breath, then spoke, "Can I take you out sometime?"

I jerked my head back. Left field was right. How had he gone from being a bossy, dominant male to softening his tone and asking me on a date? I shook my head and met his bright blue eyes that appeared confident and hopeful. "Thank you, but I don't date."

His certainty faltered and his brows came together. "What do you mean you don't date?"

I sighed. How do I explain this? "I just don't date. It doesn't interest me." And it really doesn't. Don't get me wrong, I am definitely attracted to Turner Brooks, but I see him as risk. In my head, it all played out. I would go out on a date with him. One date would turn into two, two would turn into four and next thing you know there'd be feelings. Once there's feelings, there's no turning away from them. Then commitments would happen, and what if something happened? What if he left me because he no longer cared about me, but I was still very much in love with him? What if I got a phone call or knock on the door with news that something terrible had happened to him. I'd never survive it. So I stopped it before it started.

Turner's eyebrows drew together even deeper as if he was trying to solve some mysterious puzzle that didn't make sense to him. There was nothing to solve. I readied myself for the onslaught of questions, to which I had an answer for all of them. I thought he would do what all of the men that got brave enough to ask me out would do.

Beg.

Instead, he simply nodded, smoothed his perfect features, and opened the door for me. "Okay. Well, it was nice meeting you. Maybe I'll see you around the hospital. Good luck on the job search."

What? No, "Do you even like guys? If you would just give me a chance. Are you a prude? Are you saving yourself for marriage?" Nothing. He asked me none of the questions I'd anticipated being fired in my direction. Instead, it was *me* that stumbled. Well, this was a first. I guess Turner Brooks asks once and that's the only chance you got. I couldn't tell if it was a nice feeling or a bad one that he brushed off my refusal so easily, but, regardless, I plucked a smile on my face and nodded at him. Straightening my shoulders, I moved past him and made my way to my car. I felt his eyes on me the whole way. When I climbed inside, I turned to look back at the house. The front door was closed and he was nowhere in sight. How odd. I could have sworn he would still be standing there. Shaking off my odd day, I headed home, wanting nothing more than to elevate my ankle while I soaked in a hot bubble bath and relaxed. I was ready for today to be over.

CHAPTER ONE

7 months later . . .

Annabelle

"Push, Cecile." I coached my patient.

Grunt

" . . . three, four, five, six . . . "

Grunt

The mother in labor was panting hard as she tilted forward grasping herself behind her knees.

"Eight, nine, ten. Good job, you can relax and wait for the next contraction," I said as I brushed back the hair that was sticking to her damp forehead.

"I can't do this," Cecile pleaded to her husband, who had a very apologetic look on his face. I'm sure it was hard for him to see his wife in so much pain, as it was for every husband that came in and out of my delivery rooms.

"Yes, you can, sweetie. You're doing so well," he cooed.

Tears streamed down her cheeks. "No, I can't. I'm so tired, and it hurts so bad. Please, no more. Just get him *out*."

My patient had been in labor for over twenty-four hours. The doctors hadn't been sure if she was going to dilate to the full ten centimeters she needed to in order to have a vaginal birth. The obstetrician hadn't decided whether he was going to let her progress the way that she had been, or if we were going to wheel her in to the operating room. Fortunately for Cecile, she dilated the last three centimeters in a short period of time. She had been pushing for an hour and I could see the exhaustion written all over her face. There were some moms that came in here and could continue to push for two, even three hours. Then there were others, like Cecile, where every ounce of energy was depleted and she literally had nothing left to give.

"Alright, Cecile, the next contraction is coming and the baby is right here," Doctor Linds said. "If you give me one more big push, this will all be over. Come on, give me all you've got."

She curled up into a C-position and I held onto one of her legs, while her husband held her other. She bore down and pushed until she was red in the face. I started my counting just like I did with every contraction. More sweat beaded on her forehead and I could tell she was determined to make this her last push. I looked down and saw the crown of the baby's head making its entrance.

"There you go, Cecile, the baby is coming out, keep going. Push hard!" I said excitedly.

Within a few short seconds, a bloody, wet, little baby slipped out and the doctor worked on clearing the baby's lungs and nose. The parents visibly relaxed as they looked on with teary faces. A few short seconds later, little cries sounded in the nearly quiet room. I handed Dr. Linds a couple of cloths to help wipe the baby off as he lay the newborn on the mom's stomach. This was always my favorite moment. The moment when the family of two becomes a family of three. The moment when they are inspecting every little inch of their new little bundle and they are feeling euphoric. These moments, they will never get old. After doing my normal duties of weighing, and cleaning off the baby, I stepped out of the room to give the new family some time to bond. We'd move them to a regular room once the mom's bleeding slowed down and all vitals are stable.

Walking to the nurse's station, I sat down and pulled out a couple of charts. I had to get some paperwork done before I was able to go home for the night. I was exhausted and thinking about my cushiony pillow and bed drew a long yawn from my mouth. My coworkers milled about the halls, checking on patients, and the nursery. When I started my job here, I don't think I anticipated loving the L&D floor, but I did. There was so much reward and satisfaction that came with helping to bring new life into this world. Although, my first few weeks here were rocky. I found that nurses, while friendly and extremely caring with their patients, could be a little cliquish amongst their coworkers. Coming onto a shift where they'd not had a new person in months was a challenge. It took some time, but I felt more comfortable with the nurses I worked with on a regular basis. I started charting my latest delivery and all of the medications that were administered. While I was working, I overheard two other nurses talking and my ears perked up when I heard the name "Dr. Brooks."

"So where's he taking you?" A girl I didn't know asked.

"We are going out to a comedy club downtown on Friday, and after that . . . I guess we'll see," Robin laughed.

"Uh huh, we'll see alright. Did you hear what he did with Christy down in X-ray last week?" The other nurse, whose name I didn't know, teased.

"No, what?"

"Apparently, the good doctor has a thing for supply closets. She said he didn't even give her a chance to take her scrubs off."

I glanced up just in time to see Robin rolling her eyes. "Whatever. He won't even remember X-ray Girl's name when I'm done with him. In fact, maybe Dr. Brooks will finally see the light and settle down."

The hope in her voice that she even had a snowball's chance in hell made me snort out loud. Both women turned to me and I looked back down at my papers.

"Did you say something, Annabelle?" Robin asked.

I brought my eyes back up and tried to appear innocent. "No, sorry. I thought I had to sneeze."

They both gave me an quizzical look and brushed off my interruption. "Anyway, I'm going to Pink Lace after my shift to get some things that I think he might find, *appealing*," she purred.

"Yeah, what do you have in mind?" The other girl asked inquisitively.

I peered back up through my lashes to watch the conversation. I wasn't normally an eavesdropper, but I was curious. Ever since my first run-in with Turner, I'd started paying more attention to the rumor mill. As it turns out, Dr. Brooks seemed to be a lady's man, which I pretty much already assumed. But apparently he'd made his way through the hospital staff and left a trail of swooning women. In fact,

I'm convinced that besides Robin, I'm the only one he hasn't shoved into a supply closet. Actually, I take that back. I would hope that he hasn't screwed around with Gladys, the janitor, who is eighty years old, but you just never know with people.

"I was thinking something red and silky and I'll pull my hair up off my neck. He won't be able to resist," Robin proclaimed with complete confidence.

Red silk? Sounded more like a cheap hooker color if you asked me. Turning back to my work, I blocked out the rest of their conversation. Hearing all of that brought me back to the day that he asked me out on a date. I had gone home wondering if I should have taken a chance and said yes. The attraction had definitely been there. The draw or lure, if you will, tried to suck me in to say 'yes, but hearing all of this gossip was my affirmation that sticking to my guns was the better choice. We would have had our date, and I'm sure it would have been wonderful. But I had no doubt Turner Brooks would have moved on to the next unsuspecting lady the very next day. Which was fine. Clearly that was his MO. I'd never knock a man for his game. However, since that day, I have done everything I could to avoid bumping into him around the hospital grounds. I didn't do it because I worried he wanted to ask me back out. No, I had a strong feeling he wasn't the type to ask a second time. It was more because he made me feel uneasy. There had been something I saw in his face that day, a mischievous undertone. He may be a healer, but there was a flash in his eyes that told me he liked to teeter on the edge of danger. I, Annabelle Shaffer, didn't *do* danger. Nope, I colored within the lines. That's where safety lies. I knew if I ever slipped outside of those lines, I welcomed the possibility of hurt. Because of that, I made sure I stayed inside of my protective bubble is where I controlled my future. I liked it there.

High pitched female laughing brought me out of my thoughts and I glanced up at the two women still droning on about Robin's life changing date. Blah . . . blah . . . blah. Whatever. I didn't care to listen to it any longer so I finished up charting Cecile's meds and I went to the L&D locker room to gather my things. When I slipped my purse onto my shoulder, I felt the vibration of my phone. Pulling it out, I looked at the screen. It was a text from Keegan.

Keegan: Dress shopping 2morrow @ noon.

Me: K. Should we meet at your place?

Keegan: Nah. I'll swing by n grab u.

Me: Sounds good! See you then.

Keegan and I had been hired on the same day to work in Labor and Delivery. I may have originally wanted Sports Med, but she had always wanted L&D. We worked side by side some of the time, but every once in a while our shifts crossed. Since working together, I'd become even closer to Keegan, which kind of was a rarity in and of itself. I didn't let many in. But she had this way about her. One couldn't help but trust her and love her. When she got engaged to Camden, Keegan didn't waste any time picking out her bridesmaids. I was honored that she even felt close enough to ask me. Dropping my phone back in my purse, I silently cursed dress shopping. Hopefully the other two girls would agree on what we would wear and we could focus on Keegan and her wedding dress. I also sent a silent prayer up to the dress gods that she didn't choose some Godawful color like pastel blue or purple. I didn't want to look like a cupcake.

I went out to the parking garage and climbed in my car. The drive home was a relatively short one, which tonight I was very appreciative of. Pulling into my drive ten minutes later, I let myself in the front door and was immediately greeted by my cat, Chaz. His loud purr set me at ease and all the tension from the day slowly melted away with his light thrumming.

"Hey, big guy, what have you been doing all day?" I bent down to pet his black and grey fur. He arched up against my palm and meowed at me. "Oh yeah? Sounds like you've been a busy boy." I stood back up and dropped my bag on the floor. "Are you hungry?" I asked my overweight companion, and he let out a long and low bellow. He weaved in and out of my legs as I tried to make my way to the kitchen. It was a familiar dance we did every evening. He would dart around my feet, and I would try not to step on him. I was convinced that Chaz understood every word I spoke to him. He'd been my cat since before my parent's death seven years ago and he was the only one that had been here for me when I was at my worst. I loved him and he loved me. At least I think he loved me. Unless it was more because I traded food in exchange for a listening ear. Regardless, he gave me his attention and I appreciated it.

After feeding Chaz, I went to the fridge and grabbed the bottle of merlot that I had opened the night before. Filling a glass half full, I walked down to my room, changed into black yoga pants, and a pink ribbed tank top and plopped on my bed, ready to call it a night. My kindle beside me had also become a friendly companion. I was an avid reader. I threw myself into sexy romance novels or dark paranormal ones every night before passing out. Sipping from my wine glass, I sunk down into my plethora of white down pillows and immersed myself into someone else's life. A world that wasn't my own and allowed me some comfort and solace. A place where I could let myself live on the edge and take risks. With each word that my eyes scanned, they grew heavier and heavier. My twelve hour shift had taken its toll, and the wine was quickly seeping into my blood. I hadn't even finished a chapter before I was in a deep, dreamless sleep.

─◇─◇─ ─◆─ ─◆─◇─

Before I even opened my eyes I felt a heavy weight on my chest. Then a small *tap tap tap* on my cheek. I fluttered my lashes open and was nose to nose with a very disgruntled Chaz. Looking at the clock by my bed, it read ten in the morning. Clearly I'd slept too late for his liking and he wanted to be fed, *again*. Stretching my arms high above my head, he jumped off of me and stood patiently by my door.

"You know, waking up your owner isn't very polite." He blinked as if to say "whatever." I sat up and rubbed my eyes with the palms of my hands. Geez, I must have been pretty tired. I didn't normally sleep this late, but it was always welcomed when I did. Shuffling my way into the kitchen with Chaz traipsing behind me, I fed my bottomless pit of a cat, and turned to make a pot of coffee. I had a little bit of time to sit out on the deck and soak in the sun before Keegan would be here to pick me up. When the machine beeped, I fixed my cup of Joe just the way I liked it and stepped through the sliding glass door that was right off of the kitchen. A rickety old, wooden, rocking chair sat facing out towards an empty field with a few rolling hills. I know I should probably buy new outdoor furniture, but the idea of getting rid of this chair sent me into a tailspin. As I sat down, the wood creaked as if the small frame would give way and fall apart right under me. You see, this was my dad's chair. Every morning he woke up before the birds and came outside and sat in this very spot. He would sip his coffee and read the newspaper. When I'd wake up, I'd come bounding outside and I'd sit on the railing across from him and we'd talk about anything and everything. There was a time when I used to crawl into his lap, but of course as I grew older and bigger, it just made sense that I graduated to a different spot. Daddy and I were close. I was never a girl that hated her father during my teenage years like everyone said would happen. I was the apple of Daddy's eye, and he was my favorite person on earth and he was my best friend. Of course I loved my mom just as much, but we had a completely different relationship. I was just like her. I even looked like her with reddish blonde hair and aqua colored eyes. My parents were my everything. The mere idea of trashing something that was theirs, things that were part of my fondest memories, was never going to happen. Looking out over the green grass, I watched as the clouds made shadows of different shapes and sizes, as they slowly moved on to another part of the field. I was mesmerized by the way things came and went, changing and molding to the atmosphere around it. I found it peaceful and slightly disturbing. I hated change. It was exactly why I was still in the *same exact spot*. In the *exact same chair*.

An hour passed before I decided I'd spent enough time outside in my own thoughts. I had to get moving. Tossing what was left inside my mug over the edge of the deck, I turned and went in the house. Once ready, I had just enough time to get to the door before Keegan pulled up. I picked my purse up off the ground and locked the door behind me. Keegan smiled at me from inside the car, and something about it made me relax. I hadn't been looking forward to the shopping trip, but seeing her made me remember that I enjoyed the companionship and I really did need a girl's day out.

Climbing in the car, she gave me a very cheerful, "Hey, how're ya doing?"

"I'm good," I replied. "Spent a leisurely morning out on the deck and got a little bit of sun."

She looked at me from the corner of her eye. "Yeah, your shoulders have a cute little pink tinge to them."

Ugh! I always burned. My red hair accompanied pale white skin. Just another feature I'd inherited from my mom. During the summer months, my freckles came out in full force. They annoyed me. "Apparently it's time to start slathering on the sunscreen before I spend any length of time outside. Someone remind me *why* I'm still living in the south?"

She laughed. "Uh, because the food is better and the guys are hotter."

"You've got the food part right. Maybe I should move to Seattle or Alaska where the sun barely shines. I could accept my paleness and live with my people."

"Your people?"

"Yeah . . . albinos with see through skin."

She giggled. "You're not albino, you weirdo. You do know that Alaskan people aren't as pale as you're making them sound, right? And you better not move. What would I do without you?"

"First of all, yes, there are pale Alaskans. They live way up north . . . with the polar bears. And you'd be fine without me. You'd spend more time with that gorgeous, moody man of yours."

"I think you've been reading too many paranormal books. It's the vampires that are that white. Also, time away could be a good thing. Believe me. He's insatiable."

I turned to face her. "Are you actually complaining about the amount of sex you're getting to have?"

"No, I suppose not, but sometimes my little friend down there needs a break."

Now I was the one giggling. "We work around vaginas all day and you call it 'your little friend'?

She shrugged. "Yep. But all of this brings me back around to a question I've wanted to ask you for a while. How come I've never seen you go out on a date? In fact I don't think I've ever even heard you talking about a guy."

Inevitably, I'm always asked this question. I don't announce that I'm not into dating, but people *do* take notice. "It's just not something I'm interested in at this stage in my life. I'm getting myself settled into a new job, and figuring out my long term goals."

Her voice became softer. "Don't any of those long term goals include someone tall, dark, and handsome?"

"I just don't think that's in the cards for me."

"It could be if you opened yourself up to the possibility."

I turned to look out the window. We were heading into downtown Athens, and the historic buildings were passing us by. "You make it sound like a fairytale. I like being alone."

I saw her reflection in the glass. Keegan glanced over at me with sad, wistful eyes. A hand came over and grasped my own. "I'm here. I'm always going to *be* here, even if you just want to sit and not talk." With a light squeeze she put her hand back on the wheel and focused on the road. I turned back toward her and gave her a small smile. We rode the rest of the way to the bridal shop in silence.

When we arrived, I saw that Rowan, Keegan's mom, Sarah, her little sister, and Donna were all standing on the sidewalk waiting for us. A little flutter went through my tummy at seeing Donna. Last time I saw her was the day I embarrassed myself during their baseball game. I may or may not have had a brief flash of Turner's face run through my head. I pushed it away just as another car pulled in. It was Macie. She had been Keegan's best friend since they were kids, but she has taken a liking to me too. We've hung out quite a few times over the past year, and have gotten to know each other. I liked Macie. She was loud, colorful, beautiful, and easy to get along with. But what I liked best about her was she never held back about how she felt. It's a quality that a lot of people are missing lately.

As Macie stepped out of the car, she lifted her long brown hair off of her neck and fanned herself in a dramatic fashion. "Y'all know just what kind of madness it is to get married in the middle of Georgia summer, right?"

"Yes, but there will be plenty of icy drinks to keep the heat away." Keegan stated positively. Nothing was going to get her spirits down.

"You better hope so, 'cause I swear, you keep my ass out in this heat longer than ten minutes for you to say 'I do' I'm walking."

Keegan grinned. "You'd walk out of your best friend's wedding?"

"Does this look like a face that is kidding?" She pointed to her pout. "Never mind. Who can see my face when it's melting off? Can we just get inside please?"

"Yes, please," I seconded.

As we all walked in the door, Keegan hugged everyone that was there to support her. As she checked in with one of the front desk girls, Donna gave me a bright grin. "Hey there. Annabelle, right?"

I nodded as she approached me then welcomed me in a warm hug like we were relatives or old friends. "I thought so. I'm usually good with names, but I haven't seen you in what?" She paused to think about it. "Well, I think it's been about seven or eight months."

Donna was a typical southern woman. She dressed well, with perfectly coifed hair, and flawless make-up. Living in this region of the US, most of the female population treated each other like long lost friends even if they were total strangers when greeting one another. And of course everyone hugged everyone else. Donna's small arms wrapped around me and her scent wafted through the air, covering me up like a warm blanket. She smelled so similar to what my mom used to smell like. Clean, almost like a fresh towel or sheet out of the dryer mixed with a hint of lavender. The smell hit me straight in the gut. I tried not to frown when she pulled away. All I wanted to do was bring her small frame back into me and breathe deeply.

"So how are you, honey? Been stayin' busy?" Her sweet-as-a-peach southern draw was smooth, like a fine wine.

I paused briefly to shake myself from the tears that wanted to work their way up. Swallowing down the lump that was forming, I reciprocated her smile. "I'm good, thanks for asking. Just working on the L&D floor like Keegan and taking on a couple extra shifts now and then."

"That's right. Keegan said y'all worked together. How're ya likin' it?"

Keegan started making her way toward the showroom floor and we all trailed behind her, the consultant leading the way. "It's good. I didn't realize how rewarding the work would be, but I really am happy with it."

She rested her hand on my forearm as we stepped into a wide space with wedding dresses and prom gowns galore. "That's great honey. I know the nurses that were there when I birthed all four of my boys were an invaluable asset to me. I'm so happy for you."

The mention of her sons brought my mind back to Turner. I had to admit I was quite taken by his poise, his blue eyes staring at me from across the kitchen. How his deep voice resonated in my chest. Him lifting me like I weighed nothing. He was still the most handsome man I'd ever laid eyes on. What in the world? My thoughts sounded like I had a crush on him. Crazy sauce! Someone coughed, bringing me back into the present.

"Earth to Annabelle." Macie snapped her fingers. "Do you want to try on these two dresses?"

The little blonde consultant was holding up the options and I looked them over. Both were black, and both seemed exactly the same to me. Honestly, I didn't care either way. It was Keegan's wedding, so it's her opinion that mattered more than mine, right? "Sure."

Macie went into one room with one dress, and I went into one with the other dress. What I tried on was a strapless A-line, satin cocktail number. The top was fitted around my chest, and the bottom flared out with black tulle. It was short, very light and flowy and probably wouldn't make me too hot with the outdoor wedding. I doubled checked my appearance in the mirror before stepping out. Macie was already out, standing on a podium. Keegan was up, picking apart the flaws when I came into view. Stepping up next to her, Macie looked me over.

"Should've tried that one on," she declared. "This dress is way too itchy and I don't like how the back poofs out. Makes my butt look bigger than it already is." She turned, giving us a view.

Her dress was also black cocktail dress, but it had spaghetti straps, with a sweetheart neckline. It had pleating from the waist down to the knees.

"What do you think, Annabelle?" Keegan asked.

"Me? It's your wedding. I'll wear whatever you put me in."

"Oh shut up. No you won't." Macie glared at me. Not in an angry way, but more of a "shut your mouth or I'm going to kill you" sort of way.

SLIDER

I glanced back and forth between the two of them. "I think this one is lovely and will look perfect on the three of you. Plus, we can ask the seamstress to add a couple of small straps to Sarah's dress." A warm hand came to rest on my shoulder. Donna had stood up to come to my rescue. "How long will these take to come in?"

"These we can get in pretty quickly. Three weeks should be the longest you'll have to wait." The consultant replied.

"Are you good with that, Keegan?" Donna asked her.

"Yep! I think these will be perfect. Sarah, I want to try on the one that Annabelle has on to see what we need to do to make it work on you too, okay?"

As Keegan turned to talk to her mom and little sister, Macie leaned in to whisper, "We need to plan this bachelorette party now, or it's never gonna happen."

Donna grinned at us and took a step towards the other girls. "Y'all are on your own. My bachelorette days are over."

Macie and I laughed, but I couldn't help the blush that came to my cheeks. Donna turned and joined the other girls.

I raised my arm as the consultant placed a tape measure around me and wrote down some numbers. "Do people even have those anymore?"

She scoffed. "Bachelorette parties? Well, whether anybody else has them, I don't care, we sure as hell are."

I giggled. "Oh boy. What do you have in mind? And don't tell me strippers. If there are strippers you can count me out." The little blond girl coughed, and walked out of hearing distance.

"What? You're kidding right? Strippers are a must at a bachelorette party."

"Aren't most of the strippers gay these days? Call me crazy, but I don't want their junk swinging in my face pretending like they are attracted to me, just so I will slip them a dollar bill."

She laughed. "You're probably right. Damn, now I don't know what to do."

Keegan came over to listen in. "Don't know what to do about what?"

"Nothing," we both chimed.

"Huh uh, girls. I already told y'all, no parties. Camden isn't having one, so *I'm* not having one."

Macie rolled her eyes and put her hand on her hip. "Give me a break. One of his nosey brothers is going to drag his ass to a bar or club downtown. They aren't going to let him get away with his last days of bachelorhood without going out with a bang. Don't fight me on this. I'm throwing you a party."

"You're ridiculous." She bit her lip. "What are you thinking about doing?"

Macie pointed at me with her thumb. "Well, this one over here doesn't want any gay dicks slapping her cheeks so the strippers are out." I busted out laughing. Keegan smiled but looked perplexed. "So, what if we just take you to the new bar downtown? It's supposed to be an old warehouse they beefed up to look like some California club that Ashton Kutcher owns or something. How does that sound?"

"That would be fun. When I get home I'll talk to Cam—"

"*Err...*" Macie made a car screeching sound. "Thems the brakes, missy. No asking Camden. I don't need his permission to take you out for a night of girl time and drinking. Annabelle and I will work out the day, then I will call you to let you know when later this week. Capisce?"

She sighed. "Alright."

"Don't sound to disappointed, princess, it'll be fun." Macie slapped Keegan's butt and she squealed.

"Good. Annabelle, I'll give you a call later tonight and we can discuss the details and maybe round up a few of the girls from the hospital that would like to go. Anyway," she said, effectively changing the subject. "Isn't there a wedding dress that you should be putting on?"

Keegan grinned. "Yes! It just came in." She clapped her hands. "Come on, I'm ready to try it on."

The three of us went over to Rowan, Donna, and Sarah. The rest of the day was spent sipping champagne, talking about wedding decorations, venues, food, and the dress Keegan was wearing. All of the excitement for her big day was swirling around and it was easy to get caught up in everything. By the time she dropped me off back at home later that evening, I sat in my living room, mindlessly petting Chaz and wishing I could take back my agreement to be a part of the bachelorette party. I couldn't very well call Macie and cancel, she'd never let me. But I also knew I was going to be a train wreck that whole evening. So instead of trying to shut off my overactive brain, I came up with a failsafe plan. I'd let the girls know that I was the designated driver. Limiting my alcohol would insure I was in control. At least I thought it would. With that crowd, you never know what you're getting into for the night.

CHAPTER TWO

Annabelle

"HEY, ARE YOU ALMOST READY?" Macie hollered at me from the living room.

"Yeah. Give me a sec," I yelled back.

It was two weeks later, and the girls were all in my living room. Sometime in the last couple of weeks, it had been decided that not only was this a bachelorette party, it was doubling as a slumber party. Because I was the driver for the evening, my house was the obvious choice. Now here I sat, alone in my bedroom, feeling overwhelmed. I'd been having small panic attacks throughout the day that I've had to trample back down. I didn't exactly *hate* people being in my house, I just didn't like it. I knew I was being ridiculous and letting my anxiety take control. I'd taken a Xanax about an hour ago and it was just what I needed to settle my frazzled nerves. I looked up in the mirror at my reflection and tried to conjure the girl that I once was—a carefree spirit that loved being spontaneous and wild. What stared back at me was a control freak with eyes too wide, dressed like a grandma going to church. Sighing, I stood up and went out to meet the girls.

SLIDER

There were five of us all together: Keegan, Macie, Jordan, Erin, and me. Jordan and Erin were girls from our L & D floor. They were a lot of fun and were the type to roll with the punches. Erin's a stocky girl with chestnut brown hair and eyes. Her hair was cut into an adorable little bob and despite being slightly overweight, she had more self-confidence than all of us put together. Jordan was Erin's polar opposite in looks. She was tall and lanky with long blond hair, similar to Keegan's. Except where Keegan's was wavy and thick, Jordan's seemed thin and fine, and she was a bit more reserved. I, personally, liked both of them and was glad they were able to come. Several other girls had been invited as well, but the party either conflicted with their shifts, or they couldn't find a sitter for their kids. That's what I *should* have done. I should have offered to be the babysitter so I could have avoided tonight all together.

"Alright, hookers, time to make a toast," Macie said, grabbing a couple of shot glasses and filling them up with grape flavored Vodka. I lifted my glass of water in the air. "To my bestie, Keegan. May she get completely wasted, lose her panties, and kiss a stranger tonight." They all laughed and cheered, throwing back their drinks.

"Annabelle, is that what you're wearing?" Erin asked, genuinely intrigued.

I glanced down at my floral print dress. "Yes. Why?"

Jordan and her snickered. "Honey, nobody is going to be looking at you when you have a dress on that goes to your knees, and a neckline that covers every inch of cleavage."

"Good. I don't plan on having anybody looking at my legs or cleavage."

"Why?" Jordan chimed.

I sighed. "Girls, whatever little thoughts you have conjured up in your heads, stop it. I have no intention of finding a man tonight."

"Such a waste," Macie said as she tossed back another shot. I had no idea how many she'd had, but she appeared to be happy as a clam.

"Y'all, it's not a waste. Tonight is about Keegan, not me. Besides, I'm comfortable. So can we get this ball rolling?" I argued.

"I think you need to change into something more . . . comfortable," Erin said.

"I just said this is comfortable," I grumbled.

I didn't like where they were going with this. I watched as all four of them glanced at each other and smiled. They were like a group of she-devils scheming. Whatever they were up to, I wasn't going to be dragged to the fiery pits of hell with them. I had a plan. This dress was part of my failsafe.

Keegan all of a sudden looked at me and poked out her lip. "Can I dress you into something a little more clubish? Pretty pretty please?"

"Oh my God, you've got to be kidding me? Sure, sic the bachelorette on me to make me feel guilty. Well, it's not going to work." I picked up my purse and crossed my arms.

"Come on. Just this once. I know you have something hiding in the back of your closet that deserves to be aired out," Keegan said.

"Every girl does. But I don't want to wear it."

"Can I at least see it?"

"No."

"Just let the bride see the dress, then we will go," Macie demanded.

I sighed. "Fine. I'll show it to you and then we are leaving. Deal?" I glanced around the room. All four of them made a motion to cross their hearts. I knew better than to trust them.

Thirty minutes later, they had me in the skin tight black number that I kept in the back of my closet. The top of the dress was low with a square neck that pushed my breasts up and made them spill over the material. It had capped sleeves and the length of the dress went to the middle of my thighs. I put on a pair of black pumps and then pulled my hair down, combing it out to give the illusion of soft waves. I held up my hand and drew the line with the make-up. Erin wanted to darken my eyes and add red lipstick, but I refused. Accepting that I wasn't going to allow them to take their shenanigans any further, they all nodded, finally appeased with the way I looked. I think they assumed I wasn't confident in myself or that I wasn't comfortable in my own skin. That wasn't it at all. I knew I had a great body. It's why I bought the darn dress in the first place. It flattered my every curve. But like most women, I had an outfit that was just for me. Something I kept as a "just in case" but never had an occasion to wear it. I had no doubt I would attract the opposite sex if I wore the dress. I just didn't want too. Especially not tonight when I had four other people to keep an eye on and out of trouble.

"We are fuckin' hot!" Macie all but yelled when we stepped out of the house. I would have shushed her if I had neighbors to worry about, but I didn't. The closest person lived a quarter of a mile up the road.

The girls all giggled and loaded into my car. The ride into downtown Athens didn't take very long. I may live in the country, but I was on the outskirts of the city. As we arrived, I spotted that they had valet parking. With a quick look around, I knew I'd was never going to find a spot on my own, so I went ahead and pulled up. We all climbed out and I think every male eye turned in our direction as if honing in on a prime cut of steak and their mouths were watering. I gave my keys over to a young man and he handed me a ticket. There was a line that trailed around the building and I almost got giddy. If they saw how long it was going to take to get inside, maybe they'd feel deterred enough to want to go back home. At least I would feel safe and comfortable there and not so out of control. Instead, just as I was about to turn and suggest it, Macie was talking to one of the bouncers at the door. He was eyeing her up and down and she had her hand on his shoulder. Oh no, the look on his face said this wasn't going to go in my favor. Sure enough, she whistled to get our attention.

"Let's go girls." She motioned us inside. The bouncer moved the velvet rope out of the way to let us by. Several people in the line grumbled. I didn't blame them. I'd like to know what Macie said to convince him to let us in.

As we walked up a few steps, there was a girl with a stamp pad standing in front of a cash register. We paid our cover fees and worked our way into the warehouse. The music behind the closed door was a dull thumping. The base rumbled through the floor to my feet. But that was nothing compared to how it felt when you walked inside. Standing on top of the steps and looking down, I could see everything. Strobe lights flashed in every direction and flickered off and on according to the beat. There was a large DJ booth that sat above the dance floor while several people worked up there. To my right and left were two bars. The establishment was so huge, it didn't surprise me. The sea of people in here likely required a couple of places to get drinks. Looking into the corners, there was one section that was roped off with very few people occupying the space. It looked like a VIP section. The other corners had cushioned seats that lined the walls.

The girls were bouncing in their heels with excitement. They were ready to head to one of the bars and get something to drink, while I, on the other hand, wanted to hightail it out of there and get into some comfy pajamas and cuddle with Chaz. There were too many people here. What if we somehow got split up? What if someone slipped one of the girls a Roofie and I didn't see it? What if one of them decided to go home with some random strange guy and they drove drunk? The Xanax I'd popped earlier was doing nothing to my overly shot nerves. This crowded cesspool was a nightmare. I hadn't really planned on being surrounded by this many people. When I googled the Warehouse, it showed photos, but none of them displayed this many people. This was madness. As we started to step down, I grabbed Keegan's hand. She linked hands with Macie and Macie did the same to the other girls. We formed a chain as I led them through open patches when the crowds would break apart. As soon as I reached the bar, the rest of them circled around me.

"Alright, what do you all want?" I asked.

"I say we do a shot together. Lemon Drops, y'all down?" Erin yelled over the music.

"Yes!" Keegan stated. "Why don't you do one with us, Annabelle. It will help loosen you up."

I shot her a look. She knew most of my issues, and I had a feeling I wasn't hiding my mood very well with her. Not wanting to dampen her evening, I agreed to take *one* shot. It was her night, and frankly one little drink wasn't going to cause me to lose my inhibitions. Jordan squeezed her slight frame in between several people squished together at the bar, and placed our order. Once the drinks were made and we all held one in our hands, Keegan grinned at me, letting me know I had made her happy. She knew I wasn't going to get trashed tonight, but she liked seeing me let loose.

This time, Keegan stepped up and said, "My turn to toast." We raised our glasses. "To good friends, lasting relationships, hot future husbands, and a lifetime of love." Clinking glasses, I was just about to tip my head back when something . . . or should I say, *someone* caught my eye. The other girls had yet to notice me staring, but it didn't take long for Macie to catch my line of vision.

"Well, what are the odds? Looks like a Brooks brother can be found in every little corner of this God forsaken town," she said with clear disdain.

Jordan, Erin, and Keegan all turned their heads to see what she was glowering at. About twenty feet away stood a very tall, and exceptionally well dressed, Turner. He was wearing black slacks and a slate gray button down shirt.

His eyes were looking down at the woman in front of him that was all but dry humping his leg as she danced. Personally, I wouldn't call it dancing, it looked more like she was convulsing while standing upright. His features were smooth as I took in the square line of his jaw, and the way he absently nodded at her. He wasn't listening to a word she was saying. Couldn't she see his blank expression? Despite my disinterest, I felt a pull, preventing me from taking my eyes off of him. Like an invisible tether that drew me closer even though my feet never left the spot they were standing in.

"Oh look . . . another one." Macie's disgust was palpable. For whatever reason, she wasn't a fan of the four brothers that everyone in this town seemed to know, or want to have some part of. We all stood and watched as two more barely dressed women approached. "It's like flies on shit. They just can't get enough of it."

Erin busted out laughing. "Girl, I *know* you didn't just refer to that man as shit. He is anything but. I've seen him around the hospital and I'll tell ya right now, if I ever had a chance with that man, I sure as hell wouldn't say no."

I glanced at her, as a pang of jealously shot through me. *Oh, I just bet you would.* I silently thought. I bet every woman in this bar would take a ride on the "Dr. Turner Brooks train." Everybody but me, that is. Just as the thought came and went, he lifted his head. Ice blue eyes that almost seemed to glow in the flashing strobe lights zeroed in on mine and everything around me stopped. I heard no music, I saw no woman grinding on him. In fact, I didn't even see people. In those short seconds before

Keegan stole my attention, it seemed as if I were standing alone in a room with Turner and I was seeing him for the first time after seven and a half months. But who's counting? He held me there, unmoving and unable to turn away. What happened to my indifference? There certainly *was* something about him, wasn't there. Tilting my head to the side, I watched him as his eyes stayed glued to mine. I wish I understood men more. *I wonder what he's thinking,* I thought curiously.

"Earth to Annabelle." Keegan spoke loudly into my ear. I cut the invisible line that entranced me and looked over to her. "I'm going to go say hi. Do you want to come with?"

Of course she would want to say hi. It was her future brother in law. I thought about it but decided to remain where I was. "No, I'm good. I think I'll keep an eye on Macie." It may have been an excuse, but at least it was a believable one.

"Okay, I'll be right back." She pushed her way through the crowd and approached Turner.

I watched their interaction from where I stood. She hugged him lovingly, and he responded back with a smile that was actually real. Not like the ones I saw him give the people around him that vied for his attention. He kept his hand on her lower back as he spoke closely to her ear. Their conversation seemed easy and not forced. I wondered how well Keegan actually knew Turner. *Did they hang out on the weekends? Did they chat outside of family gatherings?* I'd grown curious about him as the months passed. Not enough to go talk to him, obviously. But I did find myself occasionally thinking about him. What was it that drew so many to him?

Money could certainly be one reason, but I knew in his case it was more than that. The Brooks brothers were a force to be reckoned with. I suppose I never really paid enough attention, but now when I heard their names, I perked up and listened. Women were dying to get their hands on them, and others mourned the loss of Camden to the single world as if he had died. It really did make me want to roll my eyes. But it also plagued me with intrigue.

Just as I was about to pry my inquisitive eyes away from Turner, Keegan pointed in the direction I was standing. Oh for the love of God, I wanted to hide. What was she doing? I started to twist around to look at the other three girls. Maybe she was pointing at them. But then I saw a small tilt of Turner's mouth rise. There was no denying that he was looking directly at me. He gave me one sharp nod and then looked down at Keegan without waiting for me to nod back. That small acknowledgement was enough to cause a case of butterflies to rise up in my tummy.

Feeling frustrated by my reaction, I decided to make my way over to the others to see if they could distract me. Macie was hanging all over some guy that looked like he just came from the beach and . . . *oh my God is he really wearing a Hawaiian shirt?* Ugh, she must be really trashed if she thought this one was a winner. As I approached Erin and Jordan they grinned at me and asked if I was having a good time. I gave them an overly enthusiastic thumbs up. They must have either believed me or didn't know me well enough to realize I was feeling out of place. I awkwardly stood with the three of them and the beach bum for about ten minutes when I felt a light tapping on my shoulder. I twisted around and saw a cute waitress with a tray in her hand a vibrant blue drink sitting in the middle of it.

She picked the glass up and handed it to me. "Compliments of the gentleman." She pointed in the direction of Turner.

Keegan was nowhere around him. I didn't give any thought to where she could have run off too. Instead I found myself watching him as he eyed me from across the room. I tentatively took the glass from her hand and didn't bother saying thank you before she walked away. I watched with a raised brow as Turner lifted his own drink in the air as if to toast to me, then sipped it with a smile. I felt irritated that he was presumptuous enough to have a drink sent over to me. Only overly cocky men did this kind of crap. When he brought his glass away from his mouth, he regarded me, waiting for me to take a drink of my own. I had two choices. I could down the drink and try to act smooth and unfazed. Or I could hand it over to one of the girls, giving him the brush off, and try to ignore him for the rest of the night. Option two seemed appealing, however the shot I'd taken from earlier mixed with the Xanax was making me feel a little braver than normal. Option one it was. The ice clinked in the glass as I brought it up to my lips. Taking a small sip, a cold citrus flavor washed down my throat, bathing my tongue in a delicious tropical mix. *Mmm, it was good. Damn it!* Maybe if I drank it slowly enough, the ice would melt and dilute it. I already had that warm sensation your legs get when you know the alcohol is doing its job. I took another sip of the little blue cocktail and decided I liked it.

SLIDER

I didn't want to down the drink too quickly. Not just because I needed to keep my wits about me, but also because I wanted to savor it. There were a dozen women in this room that would fall over backwards if Turner gave them the slightest bit of attention, and for whatever reason, he was giving it to me. I knew the reality of the situation. I was a challenge. I'd turned him down. I was like Mount Everest and he saw me as something to conquer. Men loved a good game. It didn't matter though. I wasn't the hungry, little fish ready to devour the worm. If he thought I was, he was in the wrong damn pond. So I'd take his drink, allow the delectable flavor to wash through me, and I'd go about my business. Meeting his stare, I tipped my head in thanks, then turned away. I refused to give him any other acknowledgement.

Funny how that was my resolve, but over the course of the next half hour, I'd swallowed the last drop and I found myself dancing in a sea of people I didn't know. GDFR was playing entirely too loud and sweaty bodies were bumping into mine. I didn't mind though. I was in my own little world. The heat and the alcohol burning in my veins made for a concoction that had me swaying my hips. I felt amazing. And damn it if Macie didn't do good when she made me change into this dress. I was feeling sexy and confident.

"Keep it up, Annabelle, and I'll be taking you out of here and somewhere more private where not every male eye is on you," a deep voice near my ear hissed.

Twisting around to see who it was, I was slightly unbalanced. A strong hand gripped my upper arm and prevented me from falling over. Turner was gazing down at me with heat in his eyes. Those baby blues looked straight down at my exposed chest. Honestly, I'd lost track of where Turner was in the crowd and was only concerned with feeling good in the moment. Seeing him this close, and feeling him touching me startled me.

"Excuse me?" I tried to sound stern but it just came out breathy.

He clenched his jaw and his eyes roamed my barely covered body. "You heard me. You've only had two drinks since you've been here. Did you drink before you came?"

I jerked my head back and tried to regain my footing so I wasn't leaning into his hand. "No. And how do you know I've had two drinks? You only sent me one."

"I saw when you came in."

"Really?" I said with mild irritation.

"Yes."

Hmmm, what does one say to that? I was slightly overjoyed that he noticed when I came in. With all the attention he'd been getting it's a wonder he even saw past the swarm of . . . what did Macie call them? Oh yes, flies.

I pulled my arm out of his hand and stood as tall as I could. "Well, thank you for your concern, but I'm fine. Just enjoying the music."

He narrowed his eyes at me. "I can see that."

"Is that a problem?"

"It is when you're dre . . ." Turner wasn't able to finish his sentence before a blonde with long wild curls stepped in front of me as if I wasn't standing there.

"Hey there, handsome. What's a guy like you doing all alone?"

He looked at her as if she was a nuisance he would shoo away. "Actually, I wasn't alone."

She smiled up him with wonder in her eyes. Turner was apparently the answer to her loneliness for the night. Did she even hear what he just said? By the way she was inching closer, I'd say no. It didn't take long before another blonde approached but didn't say anything. I didn't understand how these women couldn't read his expressions. His face was puckered, like he'd just bit into a sour lemon.

Lifting her glass, the presumptuous one said, "I'm running a little low. Mind buying both of us a drink?"

My mouth dropped open. Turner gave her a slight head shake. "Nah, I'm good thanks."

Well, at least he was being polite.

"Awe, c'mon. Maybe it'll loosen you up enough to dance."

"I don't dance."

The one who'd remained quiet up until this point piped in, "Everybody dances with enough liquid courage." Her smile looked like it came straight from a temptress in hell.

He wasn't backing down. "Not happening."

Poking my head around the mess of curls from the first woman, their temporary distraction gave me enough time to absorb the sheer beauty of Turner. Standing this close, he had the most perfect shadowing of facial hair I'd ever seen. It was a darker color which complimented the sandy blonde hair he'd styled. Closing my eyes for a brief moment, I swear I could smell him. It was something I'd never smelled before. Definitely some sort of aftershave, which was weird because he clearly hadn't shaved, but not a cologne my nose was recognizing.

Interesting.

"Run along girls, he's not interested," I stated in an overly bold manner, getting them to realize I was there.

One with wild curls turned and sneered at me. "Excuse me?"

"You heard me." I was never one to cause a scene, but my annoyance had reached its peak.

The other blonde had the nerve to laugh. "Wow, since when did Warehouse let uptight bitches in?"

I could sense the tension flowing off of Turner and he was about to step in. No sir, this chick was making it personal now. "Probably about the same time they let easy bitches, with bad roots in. Now run along, I'm sure there are a dozen other men who are desperate enough take you ladies home tonight." I leaned forward, just to push my point. "Make sure they have their beer goggles on. Between you and me, you're both prettier from far away."

I was certain that last comment was going to earn me a slap or hair pull. Fortunately for me, Turner chose that moment to step in front of me, momentarily blocking my view.

"I think y'all are done here," he stated firmly.

If looks could kill, I'm sure both he and I would be a melted puddle on the ground the way their laser eyes were shooting beams at us. Of course, that could have just been the strobe lights that suddenly shifted to all red. Or maybe the alcohol really was getting to me.

When they walked away with their dignity tucked between their legs, Turner had a very amused expression plastered on his face. "A little possessive don't you think?"

"No idea what you're talking about."

A deep chuckle bubbled up his throat. "You might as well have hiked up your leg and marked me."

Okay, that pissed me off. Even through my nice little buzz I had going on, he wasn't going to throw around those kind of assumptions. "No, not even. I just don't like presumptuous women that think they can march around flashing their assets and can get whatever they want." I then added for good measure, "And I hate men that fall for it, even more."

I was glaring at him, but it wasn't even phasing him. His amused appearance remained. Before he could come back with something that I knew would cause me to give him a tongue lashing, Keegan came bouncing up to my side.

"There you are! I was wondering where you went." She sounded out of breath, but she looked at Turner out of the corner of her eye.

I faked a smile. "Here I am."

"What are you doing out here by yourself?" she asked.

I gestured to her brother in law. "I'm not by myself."

Her smirk indicated she knew exactly why I was out here with Turner.

"I liked the song that came on, so I came out to do a little dancing."

Her head tilted to the side. "Mhmm. And you dance?"

"Of course." I twisted my hands together. "It just takes a bit for me to get comfortable."

"Or a fruity cocktail." Turner piped in.

Clever man. I bit my lip to hide my smile. I may find him slightly annoying, but his sassy comebacks were entertaining me.

Keegan's eyes darted between Turner and me. "Uh, am I missing something?"

I shrugged. Turner put his arm around Keegan. "How about I buy you a drink, Beautiful." He changed the subject.

"I could certainly use another one," she said emphatically. Although I could tell she was three sheets to the wind and probably teetering on waking up with a killer hang over in the morning.

Turner flagged down a waitress. He handed her his credit card and said, "She's closing out her tab, put all their drinks on this."

I could have sworn she said she wanted another one. What was he doing?

Keegan placed a hand on his shoulder and got up on her tippy toes to kiss his cheek. "You're sweet, Turner, but you didn't have to do that." Turner saw she'd reached her limit as well, and she was too drunk to even notice he didn't buy her another.

Peering down at her endearingly he said, "If my brother just saw you do that, he'd have my ass, you know that right?"

She laughed. "Yep. But he's not here, so it's fine."

He shook his head. "Alright, so enough sweet talk. I think it's time to get your girls home."

"Oh it's okay, Annabelle is the designated driver tonight."

SLIDER

At least I had the sense to look guilty. Turner cocked his head to the side watching me. "Hmmm, well, that might be a problem."

Keegan's glassy eyes were trying to focus on me. "Why's that?"

"I may have pushed her over her limit," he admitted.

"Hey, I'm a big girl, I could have refused the drink."

He raised his brow. "You wouldn't have."

"Awfully sure of yourself."

"Maybe, but I know women, Annabelle."

His arrogant remark washed over me, reminding me just who he was, and what his last name was. The fun little charade was over, and I needed to remember that I wasn't interested. Based on how he sank down into his shoes, I think he realized his comment may have come across more crass than he'd intended.

Too late.

"I think it's time for that ride home now." The coldness of my voice was heard loud and clear. He effectively categorized me with every other woman in here that had approached him throughout the night. I was ready for my pajamas and my bed.

I walked away from Turner and Keegan and went to the other girls who were now doing body shots off a girl that was lying across the bar. I told them we were wrapping up our night. The bride was done and needed to get some sleep. They bitched and moaned about it, but I refused to leave them here, and wasn't going to stick around this place any longer than I had too. I'd taken one for the team, and then

36

some. I'd fulfilled my bridesmaid duties and partied hard, but I was done.

When I stepped outside for some fresh air, Turner was following behind with a very inebriated Keegan. He leaned her up against a brick wall and told me he was going to get his truck. Glancing around at my surroundings, we were the only ones on this side of the building. The air was thick with humidity, and after being in an overcrowded room, the temperature felt about the same. I should have asked the bartender for a bottle of water before I left. Leaning against the warm stone, I reached over and brushed Keegan's hair out of her face.

"You doing okay?"

"Yep." She hiccupped.

I laughed at my friend. Despite how my night was closing, I was glad I had her, and that she asked me to come. I didn't question though, that Camden would have had all of our asses if he saw her like this. The door that we'd just came out of flew open and a loud Macie, Erin, and Jordan all filed out with a couple of male tagalongs trailing. Oh if they thought they were all coming to my house, they would be sadly mistaken. Macie was about to dive into a heavy make out session with Surfer Boy, while the other man was sizing up which one of the other two girls would be a for sure deal for him. He was leaning toward Jordan when a black Escalade pulled up to the curb. Turner got out, and rounded the front of his vehicle.

"Ladies," Turner stated, but was looking right at the one about to devour Macie.

She stopped what she was about to do and childishly stuck her tongue out at him. "Party pooper." Clearly she heard the warning.

Rolling his eyes, Turner scolded, "Get in the car, Macie. I have a feeling my brother would rearrange that kid's face if he saw what you were about to do. So don't make me do it for him."

"No fun." She slapped his butt as she passed Turner, opening the back door, and falling inside.

The other two girls piled in, while Turner went straight for Keegan. He took her by her elbow and kept her balanced as he gently assisted her into the backseat. Looking around, I realized there was only room left for me up front with him. *I really should have drank more.* The two guys threw out a couple not so friendly words toward Turner before they disappeared back into the building. I stared straight ahead as he got into the driver's side and we began moving forward.

"I'm going to need you to direct me. I don't know where I'm going."

I nodded, knowing he saw. I should have thought ahead and just called a cab. I didn't like that Turner would know where I lived. I'm sure he wouldn't just show up uninvited, but it still was an uncomfortable feeling.

"Go past the hospital and take your first right."

The girls in the back were all giggling and talking about their night. I was glad they all had a good time, but I knew come morning, I'd be passing out aspirin like it was candy and bottles of water. One of the many reasons I didn't care to go out and party. Clearly my buzz was gone.

I'd given Turner a couple more instructions before he pulled up in front of my house. He parked the SUV, and got out. I went ahead of him and unlocked the door, turning on all the lights and doing a quick check to make sure that everything was picked up. I was a fairly tidy person, but you never knew if I'd dropped a pair of underwear walking from the laundry room to the bedroom. As the girls all filed in, Turner came in last, escorting Keegan and sitting her down on the couch.

"You might want to make sure they drink plenty of fluids tonight so they feel halfway decent in the morning."

"They'll be taken care of." I followed him back toward the door. The sooner he got out of my house, the sooner I could put my pajamas on and get out of this ridiculous dress I should have never worn. Plus he was making me nervous. Turner stopped just shy of the door and turned around, scanning my home.

"Nice place. How many acres is it?"

I tugged the hem of my dress, not hiding my unease. "Ummm, 4 acres."

The corner of his mouth raised in a beautiful smirk. "Damn, the hospital must be paying the nurses well."

"Oh." I shifted. "This was actually my parents place. I inherited it after they passed. I wanted to live more in the city a couple years ago, but the house was paid off so I figured I'd stay."

Way more information than he was asking for. When I saw the inquisition on his face, I knew the correct response should have been, "mhmm" and shoved him out the door. Clearly, I was a dumbass.

"I'm sorry, I didn't know you'd lost both your parents." He look genuinely sorry. But now wasn't the time or the place.

"Thanks." I was more snippy than I should have been but I was hoping he'd get the hint.

He did. "Bye, ladies. Have a good night," Turner called over my shoulder.

I walked him the rest of the way out the door. I expected him to keep going 'til he got to his Escalade, but for whatever reason he paused.

"Annabelle?"

I stood there waiting for him to say more.

"I apologize for my rude comment tonight. Call it foot in mouth disease." He tried to laugh it off. "But you're nothing like those girls back at that bar. I said the words before even realizing how they may have come across and that's not what I meant at all."

I crossed my arms over my chest protectively. "Then what did you mean?"

He looked down at his feet. Was I making him nervous? I bet he wasn't grilled by many women. "It was just me being overconfident is all. Truly, I didn't mean anything by it."

I squinted my eyes at him, not sure how to respond. He was being sincere, but I didn't really want to let him off that easy. I was having a good time. I'd allowed myself to relax a little, I'd let my guard down and accepted a drink from a man I hardly knew. That was so out of character. How quickly I let him have that little bit, and he had to blow it by saying something stupid. But I wasn't going to make him suffer any longer. I understood what he was saying, and I just wanted him to go.

"Apology accepted."

For what seemed like the millionth time tonight, Turner did something unexpected. He came towards me, pulled one of my hands away from my body, and lifted it to his lips. It was as soft as a brush of air, but I felt the warmth of the kiss all the way to my toes. No doubt my cheeks were red.

When he release my hand, he seared me with his blue eyes. "Goodnight, Annabelle."

I swallowed, hard. "Night."

I stood there unmoving as he hopped off the porch, and got into his vehicle. Even after his tail lights were out of sight, I still wasn't heading into the house. Turner Brooks was shocking me left and right. The top of my hand was still tingling from his touch, and my mind was in a state of distress. When the motion sensor light that acted as my porch light shut off, I was blanketed in darkness. Letting it wrap around me, I closed my eyes and exhaled.

Indifference, Annabelle, indifference.

There was nothing special about that man besides his looks. He was not God's gift to women, like every woman in a hundred mile radius made these Brooks boys believe. At least they weren't anything that I found worth more of my time. Giving myself a couple more minutes, I shook off the edginess that was building inside me, and went back in the house. I sought the comfort of my friends, my surroundings, and of course my cat. Time to forget about my crazy night and be the babysitter I promised I'd be.

"Who needs Tylenol?" I said, stepping inside and wondering who was going to be up first to take me to get my car.

CHAPTER THREE

Turner

"WHERE THE FUCK DID he put the ring?" I grumbled as I patted down Camden's tuxedo jacket. I swear that kid would have lost his brain had it not been encased in his skull.

"What are you doing, man?" Camden stepped up beside me. "I said it was in my pant's pocket. They're over there." He pointed at a pair of jeans strung haphazardly over the side of a chair. I walked over to them and plucked out the dainty, diamond wedding band that I was supposed to hold until the preacher asked me for it.

"Really, Cam? This could have fallen out. Ever heard of a ring box?"

"Relax, I've got this." My little brother tipped his head back and took a shot of straight Jack from a flask. I could see the nerves settling in.

Instead of giving him a hard time on his day, I gripped his shoulder and asked, "You good?"

Despite the whiskey on his breath, the smile he gave me let me know he was good. "Yeah. I get to marry my girl today. I don't think life gets much better than this."

I gave him a slight squeeze and let go. I wouldn't know. Truthfully, I'd never felt the way that he was feeling right now. Unless being in love felt the same as driving a race car,

42

sky diving, or resetting a bone that has popped out of place, I had no clue what it felt like. Not sure I ever cared to feel that way either. But I did care that Cam seemed ridiculously happy, and for today, that's all that mattered.

"Hey, asshole, you sure you want to do this?" Wrigley asked as he tried to snatch the flask out of Camden's hand.

I slapped the back of his head, causing his perfectly combed hair to shift out of place. "Knock it off. He doesn't need all the guys in here yanking his chain when he's about to get hitched. And quit trying to drink, you're not old enough."

Camden shook his head and grinned. He definitely had a little buzz going, but I was certain he'd sober up the moment he laid eyes on Keegan. "Couldn't be more sure about anything in my life."

"You're such a sap. At least my soon to be sister in law is nice to look at." Wrigley wagged his eyebrows.

Camden scowled. I stepped in front of him and patted his cheek. "Ignore the baby of the family. He was the last born and got the shit end of the stick with looks and brains." I heard grumbling but ignored it.

"Oh, hey, man, could you do me a favor?" Camden asked.

"Anything."

Reaching forward he grabbed a small gift bag that had been perched on the end of the bar. He held it out to me and I took it from him. "Would you mind giving this to Keegan? The girl's room is just down the hall. I had a little something made for her."

My brother, the sap. "Sure, no problem. Want me to tell her anything?"

"Nah. There's a note in there."

Stepping out of the room, I made my way down a long hallway. Passing several doors that were marked Men, Women, and the pastoral office, my nose tickled from all the floral scents in the air. We were a few miles outside of Athens, in the country, in a chapel that apparently had been named one of the top venues to get married in Georgia in 2015. My mother and Keegan worked like a well oiled machine ensuring that every single detail of this wedding was covered. My mother had impatiently been waiting for one of her boys to get hitched. Granted, none of us ever suspected Camden would have been the first, but Keegan was a good match for him. She was nothing like the other girls he used to chase after, thank God, and she fit in our family as if she'd always been a part of it.

Getting to the end of the hall I saw a door that had a small plaque reading, "bridal suite." I heard female voices on the other side. This must be it. Reaching my hand up, I knocked loudly. The door was cracked open and an eye appeared on the other side. It looked around then opened the rest of the way. Macie stood front and center in a short black dress looking stunning.

"He's not out there, is he?" Keegan called from a back room.

"No, it's just Turner," Macie replied.

I snickered. "Gee thanks."

She winked at me and shifted out of the way so I could move past her. "Welcome, cupcake. Boy, you clean up nice."

Stepping forward, I came inside and looked around. There were clothes, make-up, hair pins, brushes, and any other female product you could imagine strung all over the counters that lined the far wall. Two girls that I vaguely remember from the bar were dressed the same. *Must be bridesmaids.* To the right, my mother was opening a door and out stepped Keegan. She was decked out head to toe in white and looked beautiful. If she wasn't marrying my brother, I'd probably consider dating her. But she was his match, and he deserved happiness.

"Ladies," I said in greeting.

They all smiled at me as I made my way further into the room. Approaching the bride, I leaned forward and kissed Keegan on the cheek.

"If all you boys look like this, I'm in for a treat," she cooed sweetly.

"Careful, I'll steal you away from my brother. And speaking of, he sent me down here to give you something." I lifted my hand, the gift bag dangling on my index finger.

A sweet little gasp came from her mouth, and she tentatively took it from me. "That sneaky little . . . I told him no gifts." I couldn't wipe the smile off her face right now even if I tried. She was beaming.

"I raised my boy's right," my mom replied.

Keegan leaned into her and kissed her cheek. "Yes, ma'am, you did."

"Don't speak too soon, momma, Camden is the only one putting a ring on it today," I taunted her.

She beamed at me and slapped at my chest. "Oh you, hush."

Keegan, set the bag atop a sofa and started pulling out pieces of tissue paper. Every female in the room, took a step forward to try and get a better look at the prize inside, while I took a step back. This was their moment. Girls lived for this stuff. When she got to the bottom, she pulled out a little black box. Lifting the lid, she immediately brought her hand to her mouth and tears welled in her eyes. My mother pulled out the item and held it so everyone could see.

"Awe." Was the collective sound throughout the room.

"Oh my gosh, I didn't even realize that he knew . . ." Keegan's stunned words trailed off.

It was a delicate silver bracelet that had two pearls on either side of a small charm. The charm was an infinity symbol. My mom wrapped it around Keegan's small wrist and clasped it. The girls started asking questions about the meaning.

"Every night when we go to sleep, I rub Camden's back." She paused to wipe at a tear on her cheek. "I always thought he was already passed out when I'd start drawing infinity symbols on him. It was just a thing I did, I guess. He never even indicated that he knew what I was doing, or that he was still awake." She was staring at the piece of jewelry with wonder.

I'd have to let my brother know he hit it out of the park with this one. I have to admit, it was pretty clever. Who knew I might be asking for notes from my little brother's play book? I was considering this my cue to leave, but before I could the door flew open.

"Okay, I was able to track down double sided tape, but you may be SOL with the vinegar." The girls all stopped their little chatter and every eye was on a very frazzled looking Annabelle. She blew her bangs out of her face and then asked, "What? What I miss?"

It was in that moment that she locked eyes with mine, and even if someone was answering her question, neither one of us was listening. Oh this girl, there was something so very intriguing about her. I had to admit, I wasn't one to keep after someone that would turn me down, but Annabelle made the game of chase a little more interesting. The day of the graduation when she'd said no, I could see it written all over her. She was curious but wouldn't budge. That next week when I'd gone into work, I'd casually asked around about her to see if someone knew if she was dating anyone, but people either didn't know who she was, or they said she kept to herself. Since then, I'd run across her in the hospital, but I got the impression she was avoiding me. I let her. 'Til the other night of course.

"Annabelle," I greeted her.

"Hi," she said breathily.

"Vinegar?" I asked.

Her mouth moved but nothing came out. She watched me like a scared cat that just ran into a vicious dog. Did I frighten her? "Huh?"

I smiled at her to try and ease her discomfort. "You said you're SOL with the vinegar."

She shook her head. "Oh, right. Yeah, Donna wanted vinegar to see if she could rub out a stain on Keegan's mom's dress."

These women and their little tricks. "Does someone need me to run to the store and get some?"

Tilting her head to the side, I don't think she was anticipating that answer. "No, I'm sure they will find something else that will work. But thank you."

We stood there unmoving for a few more beats until one of the girls stepped in between us and took some items out of Annabelle's hand. "Alrighty, well, I'll be seeing you girls in a bit." I looked at Keegan. "And you, look absolutely stunning. My brother is a lucky man."

She beamed at me. "Thank you. And tell your brother I'm going to kick his ass for making me cry . . . but I love him."

I saluted. "Will do."

I would have said something to Annabelle before leaving, but she had effectively turned away from me and struck up conversation with someone else. Oh yes, this girl definitely fascinated me.

Annabelle

Holy hell in a handbasket, I was *not* expecting to run into Turner at that very moment. I knew I'd be seeing him at some point today, but not then, and not when I'd been running around like a chicken with her head cut off. Pretty sure I was sweaty too.

Ewww.

"Okay, ladies, it's time to line up. Everyone is seated," Donna said from the door.

Keegan shook her hands out, and took her bouquet of white peonies and pink lilies, and marched toward the door like a girl on a mission.

When we were all in our places, Keegan made sure to say something to us all. "Words can't express what you girls mean to me. That you all have chosen to take part in a day that I know I'll never forget. I'm beyond grateful, and I love each and every one of you."

"Stop it, or I'm going to cry," Macie said. "I love you, but I'm going to be pissed if you turn me into a sap before the vows are even said."

The two best friends embraced and they said something quietly to each other that only they could hear. Macie was Keegan's rock for several years before I'd met them, and their bond was special. I loved that about them.

Pachelbel's Canon started playing loud enough for us to hear, and Donna and Rowan were escorted in to be seated. Next the bridesmaids were brought in, forming a line, but spacing us out every ten or so feet. As I got closer to the front of the church, I glanced at Camden who stood completely still, with his hands clasped in front of him, and he was anxiously waiting on his bride. There wasn't a single person in this room that was going to distract him from the moment she stepped foot inside. Next to Camden was a very dashing looking Turner, whom was dressed in a classic black and white tuxedo. The whole theme to this wedding was classic, but rustic country. It was the best of both the bride and the groom. I did everything I could to keep my eyes off of Turner as I passed and stepped into my spot in front. It didn't help that I could feel his eyes on *me* though. I really wish he'd stop watching me.

When Sarah, the flower girl, came down the aisle, the music shifted to "Here Comes the Bride" and every person in the church rose. The doors in the back opened, and Keegan stood in her white dress, looking every bit the blushing bride. She had chosen to walk by herself because of her own family situation, but it didn't seem to phase her in the least. Her eyes were locked on Camden and one of the most beautiful moments I've ever witnessed passed between them. I hated weddings. I really did. If we could skip all the ceremonial stuff, and everything else leading up to it, it would be perfect. Because this right here was the only part that made me go soft. When the groom sees the bride. The look on his face is pure love. The look on her face is full of pride and adoration. This was where you knew they loved each other and this would be something that would last a lifetime. As Keegan made her way up the aisle, I kept my emotions in check, and smiled as I partook in their happiness.

If only it would have stayed that way. Unfortunately I made the colossal mistake of turning toward Camden to watch his face and I saw Turner just over his shoulder. In this light, his blue eyes looked like the Caribbean ocean. They were unique and beautiful. That same pull from the club captured me, and held me. His perfectly angular jaw, and lips that were shaped similar to a heart. He looked every bit the business man, but I knew hidden under all of that was a man that would push me to the edge. He scared me. He made me curious. I didn't want to be curious. Turner didn't belong in my bubble of safety. He was the opposite of safe. He was someone that would turn me upside down like a snow globe and shake me 'til I couldn't see past the flurries in front of me.

Look away Annabelle. I scolded myself.

"May I have the rings?" the pastor asked.

Turner was the one that cut the invisible line between us. He reached into his coat pocket and placed the ring on the pastor's palm. Macie did the same.

The whole ceremony went by quicker than I'd expected it too. Neither Camden or Keegan were super religious, so they'd chosen to cut out a lot of the stuff you'd find in a more traditional wedding. They exchanged the rings, said vows they'd written for each other, kissed and then that was it.

"Ladies and gentlemen, it is my honor to introduce to you, Mr. and Mrs. Camden Brooks."

There was some cheering and whooping in the audience. I was ready to get out of there and get some fresh air. I was certain the damn air conditioning was broken. The happy couple strode out of the church hand in hand while the rest of us filed out in couples. Thankfully, Macie was paired with Turner, and I walked with Dodger. He was eyeing her up and down as we made our way to the foyer where we'd greet everyone. I knew they used to be a couple, but I didn't know how long they'd been together or how serious it'd been.

"It's a good ass, isn't it?" I spoke out randomly.

He looked down at me. "Excuse me?"

"Well, I just noticed you checking out Macie, so I was making a remark about how great her ass was." I wasn't one to try and embarrass people but I got the impression, he was the type that could take it.

He smirked, seeming shocked by my straightforwardness. I could see why the girls were so attracted to him—baby blue eyes, and that quirky crooked smile would melt the socks off of anyone. "Busted. Yeah, it's a mighty fine ass."

I giggled. At least it lightened the mood both he and I seemed to be in. "Sorry, just giving you a hard time."

He nudged me with his elbow that I was holding on to. "Eh, no worries."

We both stopped as soon as we got into the foyer and met up with Camden, Keegan, Turner, and Macie. Turner was glaring at his brother, his eyes shooting to where I was still holding on.

"Uh oh." He leaned down to whisper in my ear, "Might want to release me soon or I may have to roll around and throw a few punches with my big brother over there. Somebody looks jealous."

My eyes flew to Turner. Sure enough, his jaw was ticking and he was holding himself back. "I'm not scared, are you?" I had no clue why I was testing him, but I didn't actually think that Turner's current expression was just because I was touching someone else. Someone that was his freaking brother!

"If you're trying to see who the strongest brother is, I can tell you that without coming to blows. Turner can hold his own. I battled it out with him one time when he was in high school, and I'd accidentally kissed a random chick in front of the locker rooms. Apparently, he'd told her to wait for him while he showered after practice, and I caught her eye." He shrugged. "How was I supposed to know he was interested?"

I giggled. "Okay, okay . . . you can have your arm back." I released him. "Just trying to figure him out is all."

"Good luck with that. Most girls try and fail."

What was it with these boys comparing me to most girls? I knew Dodger didn't mean anything by it, so I let it go. I simply responded with, "Well, unlike most girls, I'm not interested. I'm just trying to figure out his game."

He chuckled. "Again, good luck."

I decided to drop it. The congregation moved out of the church and everyone filed into their vehicles to head to the Brooks' residence. The reception was set up to take place in their expansive backyard, and no doubt was it decorated immaculately. I managed to remain unscathed and not be spoken to again by Turner during the wedding photos. I'd briefly bumped into him during one shot, to which my eyes shot to his and quickly moved away. I felt that pulling towards him even in that short moment, and I refused to be sucked in again. Most of the wedding party climbed into two different limousines to head to the party, but I decided to drive myself. Keegan understood my need to have that little bit of control and thankfully she didn't mind. I likely wasn't going to stay late because I had an early morning shift anyway.

Arriving at the house, the guests were greeted with white twinkle lights strung up in the birch trees and hanging lanterns in the willow trees. The backyard had a large tent and music was playing from speakers placed throughout the property. The DJ was busy keeping the guests entertained and the wedding party was lining up to be introduced to enter. When we all got inside and to our designated spots at the head table, Camden and Keegan immediately went into their first dance together. "When You Got a Good Thing" by Lady Antebellum was what Keegan chose. It was beautiful and absolutely fitting for them. They did all the traditional things that go on during a wedding—cutting the cake, mother and son dance, Keegan danced with Paul Brooks. He'd been more of a father to her than she could have asked for.

Standing at the bar, I had my elbows resting on the bar asking the bartender for a bottle of water when a deep voice that caused my the butterflies in my tummy to flutter up said, "May I have the next dance?"

Spinning around, Turner was a little too close for comfort. His electric blue eyes were level with mine and my heart galloped in my chest. The scent of his cologne and mint on his breath blew across my face as he gave me the most glorious smile I'd ever seen. Turner had one of his arms leaning against the bar, and it trapped me where I stood. Never mind the draw, that line that pulled me in would have kept my feet planted in their spot.

"Uh, what?" Genius response.

Why was he piercing me with those damn eyes? "I said, may I have the next dance?"

Heat crept up my cheeks and I was tempted to look down. Instead I held his eyes and said, "I don't really dance."

"Oh now, Annabelle, we both know that's a lie. I've seen you dance."

Okay yeah, definitely blushing now. "That was a rare occasion."

He bent down and spoke into my ear, "Make it another one."

I swallowed hard. Feeling tingly all over, I shook my head. He was crazy if he thought I was going to dance with him. If I was reacting to him like this and he wasn't even touching me, I could only imagine how I would be if he *were*.

"Oh come on, Belle, give my big brother a chance." Wrigley sidled up to Turner, with an identical smirk.

"You heard the kid."

My eyes bounced back and forth between them. "Why do I feel like I'm being ganged up on?"

"'Cause you are," Turner replied.

"I don't dance."

"How about a date?"

"Yeah, how about a date?" Wrigley repeated as if he were asking for himself.

I giggled. This conversation was ridiculous. "Who's asking?"

"Me."

"Me." Turner chimed in right after Wrigley. He glared at his brother and elbowed him in the ribs. Wrigley exhaled loudly with an "ooof."

"Didn't you ask me out on a date just a couple months ago?" I taunted for fun.

"Yes, ma'am. But I'm fairly certain you hit your head, not twisted your ankle."

I bit the inside of my lip to hide my smile. Why was he so charming? "Definitely didn't bump my head. My poor ankle took weeks to heal."

Shiny white teeth glistened in the lights as he flashed me a brilliant grin. "What do you say, Annabelle?"

Just before I was going to answer, Camden and Keegan strolled up hand in hand. They were glowing from happiness. Camden was laughing hard at something Keegan had told him.

"Hey you two, what's the happy couple going on about?" Wrigley asked.

Turner was drilling a whole in the side of my face with his stare. I was going to make him stew a bit longer. Plus I was interested in what these two love birds were about to say.

"Did you see who snuck into the pool house, drunk as a bunch of skunks?" Keegan asked.

"Nope."

"Dodger and Macie. Those two better put away some of Mom's breakables. I have a feeling between how drunk they are, and all that aggression those two have been taking out on each other, some things may get broken." Camden laughed.

"Oh geez," Turner said.

"He loves her," I announced out of the blue.

They all turned in my direction. My eyes got big and I raised my hands in the air. "What? I'm just saying."

Keegan stepped beside me, unable to remove her permanent smile. "Oh that boy has loved her since the day we walked into Camden's apartment. But both have a stubborn streak a mile long. They will fight their feelings 'til one of them breaks. That much we all know. Maybe the alcohol, just for tonight, is what they need."

"Or a good orgasm or two." Wrigley twitched his eyebrows.

Camden slapped the back of his head. "Do girls actually *like* you?"

"They flock to me," he said, fixing his hair.

"Right," Camden retorted.

Stepping back into my little bubble, Turner asked me again, "So about that date."

I gulped and glanced around. All eyes were on me. Keegan and Camden appeared curious as to what they missed. "Can we talk about this privately, please?" I tried to say under my breath.

"Nope."

I wanted to glare, but Wrigley jumped in again with his unwanted commentary. "Would you please put my big, pathetic brother out of his misery and just go on a date with him?"

Ever have one of those times in your life where you felt like the world just pauses and waits for you to figure out what in the hell is going on? I was in one right now. A date sounded nice, it really did. I haven't been on one in a couple of years. In fact, the last one I went on was my first year in college and I was pretty certain the guy wasn't very interested in girls. Probably why I said yes in the first place. He was safe. Turner makes me nervous. He's the furthest thing from conventional. Let's not forget he has been with half the hospital staff.

Besides the music playing around us, you could probably hear a pin drop waiting for me to answer. No pressure. Looking into his sparkling blue eyes, something in my gut said to take a leap. I may be scared, but I had a feeling Turner wouldn't do something that would make me uncomfortable.

"Okay."

His smile dropped a little. "Yeah?"

Did he really think I'd refuse?

"Yes."

That smile came back in full force. "I'll pick you up next Saturday at five."

Whoa, he wasn't giving me much time to realize what I'd just done. "Where are you taking me?"

Everyone who was standing around us scattered. Apparently they felt the need to give us privacy now. His face changed from happy to devious and troublesome.

"Don't worry about it. But you'll want to wear jeans and a tank top or something with short sleeves."

Crap. "Okay, I can do that."

He tapped his hand on the bar, and took a drink that had been sitting beside me. It looked like a whiskey and coke. "Thanks, buddy," he said to the bartender over my shoulder. "See you next week." He winked and walked away like he just won the lottery.

I looked around me wondering if anybody saw the exchange that just took place. Scrubbing a hand down my face, I sighed. Why did I have a feeling I just agreed to something that would make me question my sanity? Something in my peripheral caught eye. Turning towards the pool house, Macie came walking out, adjusting her dress and smoothing her hair back. She looked like she was thoroughly satisfied. What that must feel like . . . It'd been a long time since I'd had that. But I'll say this right now, Turner Brooks isn't getting that from me. No flipping way. I don't care how attractive he was, or how much he could smooth talk. If he thought this date was going to end in me moaning his name, he was going to be going home very disappointed.

CHAPTER FOUR

Annabelle

"A PATIENT WAS JUST BROUGHT into room 213. She's eight centimeters, and seems to be moving along quickly." One of the nurses was informing me of the patients on the floor. She was getting off shift as I was coming on.

"Okay. She the only one we got right now?"

"We just had a delivery in 215 but, I'll to wheel her into recovery before I leave. And about the momma in 213, she's an addict. We tried to stop the labor because she's only thirty-three weeks along, but it didn't work. We're still waiting on toxicology to come back with everything she's taken, but she's not in good shape. Angry and belligerent. So be careful when you go in there. We've considered restraining her."

Great. I've only dealt with one other drug addict before when I've been working. She had drank through her whole pregnancy and had started using meth in her last month. Fortunately, the baby had no ill effects.

"Okay, thanks." I picked up her chart and read through everything they knew about her. Looked like they believed she was a meth user, and maybe some sort of depressant. Wonderful. I could only imagine what I was about to walk in on. The neonatal floor was going to need to be called. Lord knew what kind of shape the baby was going to be in. "Oh," I said before she walked away. "Have they done an ultrasound to see if baby has anything we need to be worried about besides the obvious?"

"Yeah, he's just a little smaller than we'd hoped. I gave her a steroid injection to help with his lungs about three hours ago, but who knows if it will help."

"Alright." I studied the chart, received the tox report, and walked down the hall.

She was screaming before I even opened the door. Her blood work came back positive to methamphetamines and alcohol. This poor baby was going to be a mess.

"Ms. March? Hi, I'm Annabelle, your nurse." I went to her IV to check her fluids.

"Where the hell is the bitch that said she'd give me something for this pain?"

I looked up at her. "She just got off her shift. If you need something to take the edge off, I'll get that for you."

She snapped. "The fucking edge? I don't want to feel any of this. Now give me the fucking drugs."

I didn't do well with people screaming at me. "I can't have an epidural administered, Ms. March. You have too many drugs in your system that it could hurt the baby. I'm only able to give you something mild to help with the pain."

She swung her arms around almost ripping the IV out. A contraction wracked her frail, weak body, and she cried with the pain. "Give me something. I can't do this."

I left the room briefly to get her something to help control her pain, but I knew she was too far along for it to really do anything. Pushing it through her IV, another contraction hit causing her to curl in on herself.

"Get this fucking thing out of me!" she shrieked.

"Do you mind if I call you Adalyn?"

She didn't respond.

"Okay, Adalyn, I need you to listen to me. I'm going to lay you back so I can check to see if you're ready to push. If you give me everything you've got and it's time to push, all this pain you're feeling will go away."

"Then fucking do it," she growled at me.

I wished I could throw the bed back faster than it would electronically move. She was ticking me off with her attitude. I'd been yelled at by other patients, but never out of rudeness. This was just insane.

I got her flat, and checked her cervix for dilation. Sure enough, she was ready. I called another nurse to come in and assist me, and then the doctor when the baby was far enough down the birth canal. We paged the NICU to bring a team down. I wasn't trained to the capacity that I'd need for a special needs baby. When the full team was ready and set up, Adalyn pushed a couple more times and out came a tiny baby boy. Physically he appeared fine, other than he was definitely smaller than his thirty-three week gestation. But how he really was, I didn't know. The NICU got him stable in the room, and put him in an incubator and wheeled him out of the room. Chances were, Adalyn wouldn't be seeing her baby for a day or two. Not even sure she would care. She pushed him out thirty minutes ago and still hadn't bothered to ask about him.

"Adalyn, do you have a name for your son, so I may put it in his records?"

She gave me a glassy eyed stare. "I don't fuckin' care what you call him. Just give me somethin' for this damn pain I'm still in."

There wasn't much that shocked me these days, but that made my mouth drop open. "Did you know you were having a boy? We can leave it all blank for now until you figure out what you'd like to call him."

She waved her hand at me, dismissing me. "Mistake. How about that? Name him Mistake. If I hadn't gotten knocked up with the little shit, I wouldn't be here bleeding, and sore."

I gritted my teeth. Looking at the doctor whom was currently stitching her up from the small tear from pushing, he shook his head telling me to let it go. I needed a breather.

I asked the other nurse who was remaining quiet, as she cleaned up. "You mind if I step out?"

The look on my face must've said it all. "Go ahead, I've got this."

I dropped the basin I'd been holding in my hand on the bedtable and shoved out the door. Making my way to the stairs, I sat down and put my head in my hands. What in the hell was wrong with some people? I know drugs mess you up really bad, but this was beyond anything I could even comprehend. That was an innocent baby. One that wasn't asked to be conceived and brought into this world in pain. The kid was going to have a long road ahead of him. He was nameless and had a mother that was more interested in her next high than asking if he had all ten fingers and all ten toes. Sometimes I really hated people.

Turner

I was nervous. Why in the hell was I nervous. I'd been out on hundreds of dates, and never once would you catch me with sweaty palms. Wiping them on my pants for the millionth time, I pulled up to Annabelle's house and got out of the car. This girl, made me curious. I knew nothing about her except the little bit she'd let slip here and there. Women were normally very forthcoming and wanted to talk about themselves, but Annabelle didn't. Her life remained private, and it was like a scavenger hunt getting the information out of her. Knocking, she answered right away, the gust of wind from the door blowing her perfume scent across my face. *Cotton candy.* She smelled like delicious cotton candy, and all I wanted to do was taste her to see if she was just as sweet.

"Hi." She gave me a shy smile.

"Hi. You look beautiful," I complimented, my eyes roaming from her head to her flip flop clad feet. She was about a foot shorter than me, and had a tiny waist. She didn't have large boobs, but definitely a good handful. But that ass . . . and that ass in those jeans. My God, I was an ass man, and hers was perfection.

"Thank you." She stood in the doorway awkwardly, looking like she was waiting on something. "Sooooo, are we going?"

Jesus, I was staring. The poor thing couldn't even move to get around me. "Oh, yes. But you might want to change into tennis shoes. Sorry, I should have been specific with everything." She reached inside and grabbed some pink and black Nike's and held them in her hand. Okay, let's do this. Opening the passenger door, she climbed into my black Corvette, and got herself situated. "Comfortable?"

"Mhmm."

I went around to my side and started the car. The purr of the engine got me every time.

"So, you know anything about cars?" I asked, trying to drop hints where I was taking her.

She looked perplexed. "No, not really. Why?"

"Just wondering." I smiled.

"You going to tell me where we are going?"

"I will when we get there."

Her small hands were gently lying in her lap. I wanted to reach over and touch the milky white skin to see if it was as soft as it looked, but I refrained. Trees, and a few city buildings whizzed by as I drove to the south side of Athens. The radio was playing quietly in the background, and I'd only hoped she like country music.

"Okay, I want to play a little game so we can get to know each other a little better. You down?"

Her blue eyes peaked over at me. "Sure. As long as it's not too personal."

"What do you think is personal?"

"Turner." She said my name like she was scolding me. My date was feisty. Good.

I chuckled. "Okay, let's stick to the basics. What's your favorite color?"

"Green. Yours?"

"Black."

"Black isn't a color," she shot back.

"It is today, go with it. What's your favorite food?"

She paused. "Crab legs. But not any crab legs, it's got to be snow crab."

Interesting. Most girls said pizza or chocolate. "Mine is steak. Now it's your turn."

"My turn?" she asked inquisitively.

"Yes. I just asked the last two questions. Now it's your turn."

"Okay. Hmmm . . . " She tapped her pointer finger on her chin. God, she was cute. "What's your favorite cereal?"

"Now you're talkin'. One of my favorite food groups." She giggled. "Fruity Pebbles, but without milk."

She rolled her eyes. "That's a kid's cereal. I like it."

"It is not. I happen to be a very grown man, and I love the stuff. In fact, I carry a box with me everywhere for a snack."

She gave a full bellied laugh. "No, you don't. That's silly."

To prove her wrong I told her to open the glove box in front of her. She did. Right in front was a snack size box of cereal. "See."

"Way to prove me wrong." Her laugh was musical. "Don't you get tired of it?"

"No way."

"Hmmm." She hummed.

"Give me another one."

"Do you like being the oldest brother?"

"Good question," I praised. "It has it's pluses and minuses. As the oldest, I was the guinea pig for my parents. Whatever worked or didn't work with me, they did with my brothers. But I was also never babied like the other three."

"Why do I find that hard to believe?"

I shrugged. "I don't know, but it's true. Mom and Dad were hard on me and expected me to lead by example. Sometimes I wished that they would make their own mistakes and I could do what I wanted to without being watched all the time."

She nodded and the car got quiet except for the AC blowing. It wasn't that the silence was uncomfortable, but I had a feeling she preferred conversation over silence.

"You are an only child?" I glanced at her.

"How much further?" She rushed out.

Was my question to nosey? I turned my head in her direction. Trying to decide if I should push or change the subject, I thought it best to let it go and answer her.

"We're here."

She straightened up in her seat. Parking, I watched her eyes get wide as she realized where we were. I parked in my usual spot in front of the Athens Speedway Racetrack.

"Are we watching race cars?"

"No." I paused. "We're driving them." I gave her a devilish grin.

Her head started shaking and her pupils dilated. "Turner, I can't drive a racecar."

My brows came together. "Why not?"

"Because they're dangerous, that's why."

"Mhmm, that's what makes them so fun."

I got out of the car, refusing to let her keep arguing with me. I knew this was an unconventional date, but something told me, she needed this. I'd picked up on some of her discomfort when it came to pushing boundaries. Annabelle may not know this, but I've been watching her. I learned her parents died in a car accident but I still don't know if she was in the vehicle with them. She told me about the house, but I wanted to know more. I *needed* to know more. My little rule follower was going to step out of her shell for a day.

Coming around to her side I opened the door. She took my hand, and immediately released it when she stood on her own. It's okay, I planned on getting closer than hand holding later.

Annabelle stayed quiet as she followed me inside the building, and I led her out to the track where a gorgeous racecar sat fueled up and ready to go. A pit crew was off to the side and suits hung on a line near the car. I snagged one and held it out to her. She stood with her long strawberry blonde hair blowing in the slight breeze, and her arms crossed over her chest. Did she realize when she did that it pushed her breasts up on display for my viewing pleasure? I felt my dick stirring in my pants as I shifted on my feet to try and readjust. Didn't work.

"Throw this on. You want me to drive first or do you want to go?" I asked.

She flipped her hair over her shoulder in pure defiance. "Turner, you can't be serious."

SLIDER

I hid my smile and pegged her with a hard stare. "I'm very serious. Put the suit on."

Her mouth dropped. "You're awfully bossy, you know that?"

"Yes, I do. Now put it on so I can show you how to do this." She wanted to argue with me, but I was leaving no room for it. I took my suit and pulled it on. She hesitated before she mimicked what I was doing. I could have sworn I heard her grumbling under her breath. It was kind of cute. Once she was set, my old buddy from years back approached us.

Reaching out I took his hand and shook it. "Evening, Richard."

"Turner. You ready to go for a spin?" He looked at both of us.

Annabelle was wringing her hands in front of her. I wanted to soothe her and tell her it was going to be okay, but I wanted to get her alone and in the vehicle first.

"Yes, sir."

"Alright, well, the track is all yours. Pit crew will be waiting on the side 'til y'all are done. Have fun, and burn some rubber." He chuckled.

When he walked away, Annabelle leaned over to me. "Burn rubber?"

I couldn't hide my smile this time. "Yes, ma'am. That was my friend, Richard. Known him for a long damn time. He closes the place down sometimes when I want to come get some aggression out."

I swallowed. "Sounds ominous."

"Nah, come on." This time I did grab her hand. "This is an old NASCAR Sprint Cup race car. She was driven in the

Brickyard 500 two years ago and then she was retired. Pretty sure I'm one of the few that still drives her, other than Richard."

She watched as my free hand tenderly caressed the hood of the car. "And uh, is she yours?"

"No, I wish. Me and a bunch of buddies tried to buy her when they wheeled her in, but apparently money can't buy everything."

"Sounds interesting." She wasn't in the least bit interested. Annabelle was too busy trying to prevent herself from a total freak out moment in front of me.

I needed to get her in the car. She needed to get a feel for it and see there wasn't anything to be afraid of. Besides, I hadn't planned on letting her go much over one hundred miles per hour. She had no experience behind something with this much power before. I pulled her around the car to her side and told her she needed to climb in through the window. Annabelle was less than impressed.

"You're little, you can do it. Imagine being my size squeezing in there."

She giggled. "Okay you got me there." She slipped in easily. When she was in her seat, I poked my head in and strapped her into her harness. Her blue eyes were watching me intently, moving with every motion of my hands. I was careful not to linger when I got to the buckles around her chest. I didn't want her to think I was copping a feel, although I wanted nothing more than to see how she fit in my hands. Instead, I pulled away when I was done and got in on my side and buckled up.

"Okay, you ready for your lesson?" I asked.

"Doesn't look like I have much of a choice. I'm kind of trapped in here." Her side glance, and the idea of her being at my whim was more of an aphrodisiac than it should have been.

Giving her some peace of mind I told her, "You want out at any time, just let me know. If I'm going faster than you're comfortable with, let me know. If you need *anything* just let me know, and I'll stop."

She brought her bright round eyes to mine. It was a moment, connecting and building a sense of trust in a matter of a couple second. She nodded giving her approval.

"So for starters, I'm going to pull up to the start line. When you're in this seat, you're in control of everything. The car will not move unless you are in gear and you are the one pushing on the gas. It's just like any other vehicle other than there is an engine in it that has 900 horsepower. It's powerful Annabelle. I want you to understand that." She was listening to my every word with rapt attention. "This vehicle can get up to 200 MPH. We are in a roll cage and are quite safe, but you have to know how to handle this thing around the corners. You shift it just like any other car. Have you driven a standard before?"

She slowly shook her head.

I grinned. "No, no big deal. Alright, you ready? I'll take the first lap slow. After that I'm going to open her up."

Pushing the gas I felt the familiar purr of the engine. I'd driven this car more times that I could count. I knew it well. Creeping up in speed, I was still on the straightaway. The bleachers were breezing by, but I had tunnel vision. Shifting, I kicked it up a notch. I was creeping up to 90 MPH just as I was hitting the first corner. Annabelle's hand came up and she was about touch my forearm, when I downshifted and slowed before turning the wheel. She dropped her hand into her lap. I wanted to look at her and tell her it was okay, I was going to keep her safe, but I had to keep my eyes on the track. These cars were unpredictable. I would have spoken to her, but the engine was too loud.

We took both corners at about the same speed. The second one, she kept her arm down and gave me the trust I was silently asking for. I'd only hoped she was enjoying herself just a little bit. As I hit the end of my first lap, I was ready to open it up. I wanted to feel the adrenaline pumping in my veins. I knew it was probably not the wisest choice to give it what I normally did, because I knew she was already on edge. If I wanted Annabelle to feel comfortable, I'd need to take it easy. When I started the second lap, I pushed on the throttle harder than the first time. I let the speedometer creep up to 100 MPH. Even at this speed, you can feel the force of the G's pushing you back into your seat. Instead of bringing it down to a comfortable speed for her when I got to the curve, I only downshifted once, and kept up the momentum. Surprisingly, she didn't freak. Maybe she was okay with this after all. I continued on the track and at the end of the lap, I came to a complete stop in the pit. The crew immediately began fueling the car back up, and checking tire pressure. I looked over at Annabelle, and she was staring at me with such wonder in her eyes. Never had a woman looked at me like this.

"You doing okay?" I asked.

She didn't answer right away. It was like she was trying to find her words. "I've never gone that fast before."

"It's a different feeling isn't it?"

"It is."

"Would you like to drive? I can teach you." I wanted her to so bad. I wanted to see her let loose and mesh with the car. It would have been the biggest turn on. But I could see her answer already.

"No, I'm okay. I don't know how to drive a stick and I'm sure they don't want to replace the transmission on this thing if you try to teach me. I'd rather just sit and *feel* if that's okay?" She hesitated, expecting me to push her into changing her mind. I wasn't.

"That's fine." I smiled to offer reassurance. When she smiled back, the feeling that shot through me was incredible. I wanted to make her happy. I'd never given two shits about other women I dated, it was always about making them make me happy. But that smile she gave me, my God, it could light up a room.

We ended up going around the track about ten more times before calling it quits. I pushed the car and her comfort level to about 140 MPH before Annabelle, did in fact reach over and touch me. She'd had enough and I'd maxed out her level of comfort. I was fine with that. After we'd taken off the suits and we were walking back out to my car, I grabbed her hand. Rubbing my thumb back and forth over the smooth skin on her wrist, she was as soft as I'd imagined. Getting her settled in, we drove the whole way to her house in silence. The only thing I asked was if she wanted something to eat. She said she wasn't hungry, and I knew what she meant. It was almost as if both of us were trying to take in the evening we'd just had. As soon as we arrived at her house, I helped her out and walked her to her door.

"I hope you had a good time," I said uneasily.

"Mhmm, I did." She glanced down shyly.

"I'd like to take you out again, if that's okay."

She pondered it for a moment and then said, "I'd like that."

There was no stopping the smile that spread across my face. "Alright then. I'll be in touch. I need to think about where I want to take you next."

Her eyes got big. "No more dare devil stuff." She laughed. "Not sure my poor heart can take it."

"Did you get hurt today?"

She was confused. "Well . . . no, but . . ."

I cut her off. "Did you have fun?"

"Yes."

"Okay, I'll let you know when I've got the next date set up. And Annabelle . . . it *will* be fun."

She sighed, knowing she wasn't going to win. "I'll wait for the call then."

Leaning forward, I tenderly kissed her cheek. The scent of cotton candy was lingering on her skin. I heard her small gasp and I wanted to kiss her on the mouth, but some things were better waited on. Next date, I was going to take what I wanted.

"Goodnight, Annabelle. Thank you for a good evening."

"Goodnight, Turner." She twisted in her cute little tennis shoes and went into the house.

SLIDER

She's different. I'll give her that much. I was very intrigued by her. I was going to need to think of something that I could do with her, something that we could actually sit and have conversation. Unfortunately, the race car was too loud for either of us to hear the other person. This was going to take some thought on my part. I wanted to break her out of her shell and see what she was made of, but I could tell it was going to be a process. Annabelle was my new project, and I was looking forward to seeing who she really was.

CHAPTER FIVE

Annabelle

I WAS STANDING OUT IN FRONT of the PAWS animal shelter waiting for Camden and Keegan to show up. They were thinking about adopting a dog. Keegan had called and asked if I wanted to join them and maybe get lunch afterwards. I reluctantly agreed. My date with Turner was almost two weeks ago and I had kind of kept to myself since. I had a feeling she wanted to pry and find out what happened. Why couldn't she just ask Turner? I'm sure he'd tell Camden if he asked. Keegan had called the day after, but I was still processing the fact that I had actually enjoyed myself.

Speaking of, they pulled up a couple minutes after I'd parked. Getting out of their car, Keegan looked like she was still glowing from her wedding day.

"Morning," she said.

"Morning back." I smiled at her.

Camden stepped beside me and nodded. Such a conversationalist.

"Alright, let's do this." She rubbed her hands together. "And, for the love of God, I am going into the cat room whether you like it or not." She fixed him with a pointed stare.

He flung his hands in the air. "Fine, we'll go into the cat room. But don't get pissy with me when I walk out sneezing or my eyes are itchy."

She leaned in and kissed him sweetly. "You'll be fine. But thank you."

"Welcome," he grumbled.

As we walked in she whispered to me, "He says he's super allergic to cats, but I have yet to see a reaction from him when we've been somewhere with a cat."

"Sneaky. Clearly not a cat lover." I giggled.

As we walked in, we were greeted by the workers who asked us to fill out some information forms. Apparently they don't let just anyone in here. And who knows, maybe I'll come back for a friend for Chaz. When we were done with that, we were led into a side room where barking dogs galore were behind closed doors and waiting anxiously for any human to stop and say hi. The first couple of dogs were older, and lazily sat in their rooms with disinterest. Another room held a beagle mix whose tail was nonstop wagging. She was very cute. Camden and Keegan put her down as a maybe. Little dogs and large ones were scattered throughout and still, they hadn't come across one that seemed like "the one." As they approached the final room and feeling discouraged, they came across a black lab with a white patch on his chest. He was a six month old baby, who had been born at the shelter. Letting the volunteers know, they pulled the pup from the room and let Camden and Keegan go into a separate room to get to know him.

While the playful little guy chewed and nipped at Camden's hands, Keegan turned her attention toward me.

"You haven't told me much about your date with Turner. Spill the beans. You going on another one? Was he a gentleman? And race car driving . . . that shocked the crap out of me. I had no clue you were even into racing."

I held my hand up to her. "Okay, for starters, slow down. One question at a time. He was a gentleman."

Camden snickered in the background. "Well, that's kind of shocking. You all thought I was a brut, Turner is worse than I ever was."

Keegan nudged him. "Hush. She's talking. Anyway, you were saying?"

I glanced back and forth between them. Their relationship and sweetness made me envious.

"Yeah, so I'm not in to racecars. In fact, I had no idea he was even taking me to the track. Had I known I would have told him he could take his idea of a good date and shove it up his ass."

Keegan's eyes got wide. "Then what made you agree to do it if you didn't want too?"

"Honestly, I don't know. He pulled into the parking lot and he gave me a look that made me feel like I could . . . I don't know, trust him? So I went with it."

"Wow. I'm honestly kind of shocked."

"Did you enjoy it?" Camden asked inquisitively.

The puppy was vigorously running around the room, tossing toys in the air and making them squeak.

I thought about how to best answer him. "Yes, I enjoyed it. At first, I was terrified. I'd never been inside a car that could go that fast. Turner ended up going around once, showing me that he had complete control of the vehicle. I know he wanted to push it to the limits, but I wasn't having it."

I closed my eyes and remembered how the wind whipped around me and everything breezed by so fast I couldn't make out shapes. What I remembered most though, was the way Turner looked at me, letting me know he had me. I knew when his blue eyes met mine, he was going to keep me safe. He didn't even have to say anything to me, I just knew.

Camden chuckled. "Turner always was the one to push the boundaries."

"What do you mean?"

"When we were kids he was always the first one on the roller coasters, or jumping off the roof of the house onto something. I thought Mom and Dad were going to give him up for adoption or give him away on a street corner."

I tilted my head to the side, more curious than before. "So he's a bit of an adrenaline junky?"

"Yeah, you could say that."

A worker popped her head in. "How's it going?"

"He's amazing!" Keegan clamored.

"He's a sweet boy. Would you guys like to see any other dogs?"

Keegan and Camden looked at each other. "There was a female we saw, but it seems like Cam really likes this little guy," Keegan told her.

The worker beamed. "Well, if you'd like, I can start processing his paperwork while you speak to one of our adoption agents and they can give you all of his info if you are still interested."

"That would be great, thanks," Camden agreed. He was holding the puppy on a leash, and I could tell this was the little fella they were going to go home with today.

When the worker closed the door, Keegan turned back toward me. "Okay, so now what? Are you two going to go out on another date?"

"I agreed to a second date. I just don't know where he's taking me."

"How exciting," she shrilled.

"Calm down, Keegan. It's just a damn date. Not like they are walking down the aisle," Camden scolded.

She slapped his arm. "Shut up."

I shook my head. "Definitely no weddings for me. This girl has vowed to live the life of singlehood."

"Why?" Camden asked, completely contradicting what he just said to Keegan a moment ago.

I stared at him. "Because I'm not interested. You become so invested in someone, giving your full self over to another person, and then what? What happens when they die? What would you do? How do you go on? I'm sorry, but I'd rather not go there."

Keegan looked sad. "Didn't know you felt that way."

"It's called self-preservation. I don't knock anyone who gets married and has a family and all that, but it's just not for me. I decided this a long time ago."

Technically, it wasn't that long ago. Around the time of my parents death I made a vow to myself that that if I didn't give my emotions to another, I'd spare them the grief and agony if something ever happened to me and vice versa. I didn't care that most people didn't get it. In fact, it's why I rarely ever spoke about it. Everyone who has met me since my parent's accident just thinks I'm some indifferent cold hearted bitch or a lesbian. When the reality is, I'm neither.

"Oh, can we change the subject for a minute?" I asked. Refusing to actually keep talking about my date and love life.

"Sure, what's up?" Keegan replied.

We were being led out of the puppy play room and Camden was greeted by one of the adoption agents. They were currently going over the puppy's records, while Keegan and I sat back and chatted.

"You sure did miss some action the other night."

"Oh yeah? What happened?"

"We got a mother in that was a severe addict. Any drug you could think of, it was in her system. She was so awful—belligerent, yelling, and the worst part, she didn't care about her son she'd just given birth too. I'm hoping in all the years I'm a nurse, that's the worst that I see."

Keegan's eyes were wide. "I heard about that one. Didn't know you were the delivering nurse. When was this?"

"My shift right after the wedding."

"How's the baby?"

I paused. "Actually, I don't know. I had planned on stopping in to check on him yesterday, but was beat after I clocked out. I think I'll head into the NICU tomorrow before I go in. He was such a little guy. Hoping he's a fighter."

She rubbed my arm. "No doubt. And it's probably a good thing I wasn't on that day. Lord knows I would have throttled that woman."

"Oh, it took everything in me to not grab her by her face and say, 'wake the hell up, your baby needs you.' Of course I didn't and went and blew off some steam in the stair well. Speaking of, someone really needs to put a dart board in there. Sure would help when I'm catching a breather."

She giggled. "Definitely."

"Hey, baby, I need you to come over here and sign some papers," Camden called for her.

Awe, puppy time for the happy couple. I took a step back and let her go be with her husband. Heading to the cat room, I sat down as the little purring furballs surrounded me. Sighing I thought to myself. *Ah yes, destined to forever be a cat lady.* I didn't know if that made me happy, or sad. Either way, it's how it was going to be.

Turner

Sitting in my office on the fourth floor of the hospital, I was staring out my wall of windows instead of doing the paperwork that I was desperately behind on. This was ludicrous. It had been almost two weeks since I'd taken Annabelle out on our first date, and I had yet to plan our next one. Things in the operating room had been hectic, and I barely had any time to myself, let alone trying to schedule something. I felt terrible. Even worse, I had a fucking hell of a time concentrating on anything that didn't have to do with her.

SLIDER

The one time I'd managed to pick up the phone, her line had just started ringing when I had been called out to an emergency surgery. I've been frustrated. So frustrated, that one day not too long ago, I found myself down on her floor, outside the nursery window, peeping in on her like some creeper. I'd watched as she tenderly gave a newborn its first bath. There were other nurses in the room, and a couple had taken notice of me, but thankfully none of them tipped her off that I was around. I watched her for a couple minutes and decided it was best to leave. I'd considered poking my head in to see how she was doing since we hadn't spoken, but it didn't seem like the time or the place to do it. Women got all weird being around babies, and I swear it was like you could hear their ovaries exploding when they saw, heard, or smelled a newborn. I didn't want any part of that. Instead, I went back to my office, called her cell phone, and left her a message apologizing for being MIA for so long. I'd consider myself lucky if she actually called me back.

I was relentlessly clicking my pen when my cell on my desk buzzed. I sighed. Whoever was calling was going to get the not so pleasant side to me. I was *not* in the mood to shoot the shit or talk. Picking it up, I looked at the screen and stopped in my tracks. It was her. Jesus, she was the last person I was expecting to hear from.

"Hello, Annabelle."

"Hi," she responded.

"You must've got my message?"

"I did," she stated matter of fact.

I twisted back and forth. "Good. I apologize for not getting back to you sooner. I tried calling a while ago, but timing didn't work out to well."

"Apology accepted. Everything okay up there?"

"Yeah, just busier than normal. Kids are busting their asses at football practice and coming in left and right with injuries. Regardless, I have a day off on Friday. You working?"

"I'm pretty sure I'm off, let me check."

She was rustling through some papers, when she finally came back on the line and said, "I'm free."

I smiled. "Okay, I was thinking we could do something a little more active this time. You down?"

"Turner," she said with a tone that dared me to not push her limits again. Too bad, Princess, it's happening.

"No race cars or tracks this time, I promise. Just light walking, and fresh air."

She stayed quiet for longer than I'd hoped. I was about to ask her if she was still there when she responded, "No race cars?"

Annabelle's sweet voice caused things to stir under my scrubs. "Cross my heart."

"Alright. When will you be by to get me?"

I thought about it. "I'll be by around eight in the morning. And again, dress casual."

"Sounds good."

"See you soon, Annabelle." My voice was deeper than before.

Her breathing was a little heavier. "Bye, Turner."

"Bye."

SLIDER

I hit "End" on my phone and set it on my desk. It was most definitely wrong that I led her to believe that this was going to be a docile outing. But I didn't care. On this date, she was going to have plenty of time to talk to me and tell me more about herself. I also didn't mention that she wasn't going to be able to get too far away from me either if conversation got to be too much for her. Come to think of it, she may hate me by the end of Friday, but at least I will have spent the time with her that I was in need of. Now, it was time to make a couple of calls and get this shit set up.

CHAPTER SIX

Annabelle

TURNER HAD PICKED ME UP almost an hour ago and we'd been driving west for quite some time. I had no clue where he was taking me, but we were definitely headed into the mountains. I did my very best to hide my discomfort with the twists and turns and being this high up. Turner didn't know that my parents had died on a windy mountain road, and I didn't plan on telling him either. He made a turn into a national forest preserve and drove back a couple of miles. When he parked, I looked around. All my eyes could see were pine trees, and a creek that ran next to a paved trail. There were no signs indicating what he had planned for us. I started to wonder if it really was going to be a low key date and maybe he knew of a spot that we would walk too and sit and talk. Oh God, talking. Just as scary as riding in a race car.

"You ready?"

"Mhmm." I stated, "I have never been here before."

He smiled a dazzling grin at me. "I haven't either. Let's go."

He hadn't been here before? Then how in the world did he know where he was taking me? I'd assumed he was taking me on a hike or walk. Maybe a friend or one of his brothers told him about this place and he was going to see if we could find it together. I didn't wait for him to help me out of his Jeep. Yes, this time he picked me up in a two-door, Jeep Wrangler. It was lifted and had massive tires on it. He helped me up into it when he picked me up. Getting out of it, there was nothing graceful about it. You simply *fell* out. When he got to my side, he chuckled.

"You alright there?"

I stood straight. "I'm good."

He took my hand with no hesitation and led me to the trail. Turner had a back pack with him and I wondered what was in it.

"You have some sort of weapons in there you plan on massacring my body with and burying me out in these woods?"

He burst out with a full bellied laugh. "No, but that was creative, I'll give you that one."

I slowed to give a small bow.

"I have some snacks and a couple water bottles in case we get hungry," he answered seriously.

"Gotcha."

"So any clue where we are going?"

"Not a single one."

"Perfect."

He wanted me in the dark. This trail we were walking on was beautiful. Wild flowers lined the edges of the path and the water running through the creek bed was so serene it made me want to sit and stick my feet in it. We walked around a corner and a wooden sign was off to the left with a couple arrows pointing in different directions. Up ahead, the pavement split in different ways. As we approached the split, we took the path that made my stomach drop. It was titled, "The Gulch Zip Line."

What. The. Fuck.

"Turner, what are you having us do?"

He was kind of pulling me along now. "It'll be fun. Trust me."

Trust. That was a huge word that, frankly, was tossed around and definitely not given freely by me. You had to earn it. There was a building that looked like a forest ranger cabin a few yards in front of us. You'd never even know this place was here unless you knew where to look. Literally, our whole drive, not one sign mentioned zip lining. The log building was small and square, but when we went inside, there were a couple televisions that lined the walls with images of groups wearing safety gear, posing for the cameras and having fun. Turner released my hand and went to the counter.

"Hi, we're here for a private guide," he told the person sitting behind the counter.

"Yes, sir. We were expecting you." She pulled a couple papers from a plastic organizer in front of her. "I just need you both to fill out these forms and sign the waiver on the back. We can get you all set up after that."

Turner shifted to look at me. I stepped up beside him and looked at the stuff I was supposed to fill out. Most of it was standard information. The one that made me pause, was the paper that basically said they assumed no responsibility if death or injury occurs while on the course. So, was I supposed to just sign my life away?

"Uh, ma'am?" I asked.

"Yes?" She smiled like nothing about these things was odd.

I tapped the paper with my pen. "This one right here. Umm, can I ask how often, if something does happen, does one get hurt while doing this?"

She shook her head. "Oh, it's just a basic form. But I can tell you, in the two years that I've worked here, we've only had one accident, and that wasn't even because the person was on the course. They hadn't taken their meds and went into diabetic shock from low sugar levels."

Did she not realize this was still not reassuring to me?

"Okay, but what kind of things could happen while doing this?"

Her head tilted to the side, and she was totally perplexed by my question. "Well, I suppose anything. Accidents do happen, but I assure you, the whole course is safe. One of our guides goes through it first thing in the morning checking the lines and making sure that everything is tightly bolted to the trees. It really is very safe. Just try to relax and have some fun. Almost everyone that comes through here is nervous in some way, shape, or form. You've got this."

Her pep talk sucked. I just wanted to clip her onto one of the lines in the trees and fling her down it while I yelled profanities about her crazy ass.

Turner remained quiet while I had my freak out with the poor worker. I was surprised he didn't jump in and try to settle my frazzled nerves. Honestly, it was probably for the best. She was a stranger to me and I wouldn't lash out at a stranger. If he had tried to speak to me, I would have punched him in the arm. Not that the big guy would even feel it.

I went ahead and signed the papers, even though I truly wanted nothing more than to take off running back in the direction we'd just came. After I passed them back, we were instructed to go into a side room where helmets, straps, and all sorts of other contraptions were hanging from the walls. A male worker, named Joe, helped fit us into the proper gear. He explained to us what the straps were for, and how we were going to sit in the harnesses when we got to the first platform. I slipped my helmet on my head and I could feel heat creeping up my cheeks. I'm sure I looked ridiculous. But when I glanced at Turner, he winked at me. A couple little flutters went through me and I looked down at the ground. I saw his feet come into my line of vision and a finger tipped my chin up, forcing me to look at him. He stood too close. And why in the hell did he look so good with such a dumb hard hat?

"I see your thoughts flying across you face. You're beautiful."

The crystal blue of his eyes and the heartfelt tone in his voice, I had no choice but to listen.

"Thank you. You're sweet."

He leaned in and spoke into my ear, "And you are even sweeter. Seriously, you smell like cotton candy every time I'm near you and I'm beginning to wonder if you taste like it too."

He stepped back from me and directed his attention to Joe. Okeydokey, now how was I supposed to respond to that? My heart took a hiatus for a solid ten seconds, while my underwear felt entirely too damp. There I was nervous about this rope course, but the man who stood next to me caused

SLIDER

reactions inside me that I'd never felt before. He was more dangerous than I had given him credit for.

Swallowing hard, I pushed my thoughts aside and followed Joe and Turner out to the path behind the building. There was a white van that I guess we were supposed to get in to. We drove up a mountain side that seemed like a straight shot up from where we'd just come from. I was going over every possible thing that could cause me to fall to my death. And also, who would take care of my poor Chaz if I died? I truly felt like these were legitimate concerns. Once at the top, Turner filed out and I followed behind him. I know he wanted to grab my hand, but was likely picking up on my vibes that I wasn't really in the mood to be touched. I needed some space so I could breathe through this. I didn't know what I was going to do when I had to make that first step off to free fall. If that's what you'd even call it.

We walked to a wooden platform where a wire cable hung across the top of a forest. Okay that was a seriously long drop. This was crazy. Turner was crazy. *This was crazy.* I'd rather be in a race car right about now going 140 MPH, not getting ready to fling myself off this platform and expect these wires to hold my happy ass long enough 'til I'm on the other side.

"So, let's go over a couple of things," Joe said, in a serious tone. "The other guide is already here, and she is down on the other end waiting to meet you both after your first jump. I want you to hold the wire in the back, never in the front. You hold it up front, you could lose a finger. At the end down there, you'll see a block. It will help slow you down so you don't go speeding into poor Serenity." He chuckled at his

90

own joke. "She's sturdy, but I think she'd move before she lets y'all run her over."

I wasn't laughing, but Turner found it humorous. I glared at him. When he caught my expression, he wiped his smirk away. He mouthed the word "sorry." I just shook my head at him. He winked like it was going to get him out of hot water with me.

"Okay, who's going first?"

"I think Annabelle needs to go."

"I think you're on crack, Dr. Turner," I snapped.

Joe was now laughing at my joke, except it wasn't one. "Okay you two. Annabelle, step up to the plate."

I did as he asked. He took hold of my karabiner and hooked me in. He yanked it twice and released me.

"So quick question," I said with a slight quiver to my voice. "Can this thing actually hold me? I mean, I haven't gone jogging in a while, and I haven't exactly been watching my figure."

Turner's hand brushed mine. He was trying not to laugh.

"These clips and cables are capable of holding over one thousand pounds. I promise, even if you didn't hit the treadmill this morning, you're very much in the clear."

"Well, looks like I'm going whether I want to do this or not."

"Put your faith in the free fall, Annabelle. You're going to be fine. Just watch for Serenity's signals at the bottom. She will let you know when you need to slow yourself down. I'll meet y'all on the third platform."

I nodded. Sitting down, I let all of the equipment hold my weight. I oddly felt very secure. But that could be deceiving.

Joe said he was going to count down from three, after that I was supposed to step off.

"Annabelle," Turner called my name.

I twisted, giving him an expectant look. "Hmmm."

"Before you go, tell me something about yourself. I don't care what it is, just tell me something."

Slightly taken aback, I thought about what I wanted to say. Something about myself. I never really talked about myself, so thinking of something to share wasn't the easiest task. Couldn't he ask me another question? Joe started his count down.

"Three . . ."

Seriously, what did he want to know? I felt like everything was too personal.

"Two . . ."

We just played the question and answer game in the car. Didn't we share enough? The man eats cereal for a snack for heaven sakes.

"One . . ."

Pressured, I blurted the first thing that came to mind.

"When I was a kid I always wore dresses so the boys could see my underwear when I hung upside down on the monkey bars." And with that I jumped.

I didn't wait for his response. I wanted to get away. The only option I had was down. I was fully expecting a free fall. The kind where your tummy drops and you feel like there's no sense of gravity. That wasn't the sensation at all. It was more like being on a roller coaster without the drop. The wind was in my hair and the tree line below me whizzed by. I briefly glanced back and saw Turner grinning ear to ear.

And did he just fist bump the guide? I caught some serious speed and my mind told me it was time to slow down. I watched the bottom of the line where the next platform was in place. There was a woman there, waiting for me. She started giving me hand signals letting me know I needed to reach up and grip the wire. I did. Even though I wore a leather glove, I could still feel the heat through the material burning my hand. My momentum slowed and there was a wooden block that my harness hit making me slow faster than if I tried to do it on my own. Serenity hollered out to me to put my feet down when I got to the platform. It was all a matter of seconds that everything happened. I planted my feet, and stumbled forward, while Serenity grasped the top of my line and made me come to a complete stop.

Holy adrenaline.

"How was it?" she asked. Serenity was a tall brunette woman, I would guess to be in her early thirties.

"I haven't decided just yet." My hands were shaking and my heart was palpitating.

"Just wait 'til you get to the third line. You'll have some decisions to make." She wagged her eye brows like what she said would impress me. All it did was freak me out.

Did she know I was terrified of this stuff? Surely not or she wouldn't have said what she just did. I didn't acknowledge her. Instead, I looked at the top of the hill where I'd just come and watched as Turner began his slide down. How did he make this look so graceful? He had his arms out wide and his head back like he was enjoying every second of the ride. I was slightly envious. What it must feel like to let go like that.

SLIDER

When he got to where I was, his smile looked like a permanent fixture on his handsome face.

"God, that felt good." Serenity unclipped him. "What did you think?"

Did the man realize his harness snuggly fit him and I saw everything he was packing? I did my best not to look, but holy crap I could see where he would be slightly confident in the man whore department. Clearly he had a reason to strut his stuff. *Focus Annabelle.*

"Uh, I uh . . . " Clearing my throat and closing my eyes for a brief moment to gather myself, I opened them and met his crystal blue eyes head on. "It was an interesting feeling."

"Interesting good, or interesting bad?"

"Interesting, and I'll leave it at that. There are how many more of these things? I'll let you know when we are done."

He chuckled. "Okay, fair enough."

I nodded.

"So you wanted the little boys to see your underwear, huh?"

Oh God, I was so caught up in everything that I forgot I spit that little bit of knowledge out. My cheeks felt warm, and I bit my lip hard, trying to hold my composure. Why must he talk about embarrassing things when I have no place to escape too? Probably part of his plan, the asshole.

"I was under pressure. You asked and it was the first thing I could think of. Don't judge." I snapped, trying to hold back an embarrassed smirk.

He held his hands up in surrender. "Hey, I'm not judging. I am just shocked is all. Let me guess, you wore those cute little 'days of the week' underwear too."

My eyes got wide. "What did I say about judging?"

Turner burst out laughing. "It was a wild shot in the dark. I had no clue you really did."

I slapped at his arm. "Alright, sir, turnabout is fair play. Tell me something about you."

"Let me think about this one."

I shook my head. "Oh no. You don't get to think about it. You made me answer under pressure. Well, here's your pressure, Mr. Tell Me Something. Three . . . two . . . one."

"You drive a hard bargain, Annabelle. Okay, I almost joined the Navy before I headed off to college. I wanted to become a Navy SEAL."

Whoa, I was slightly impressed. "Why didn't you?"

"Another question, another line. Let's go, pretty girl, ask me at the bottom."

Serenity clipped Turner onto the next line of the course. "Ready to go!" she announced.

He took no time flinging himself off the edge. This section seemed a little shorter than the last one. He did this so carelessly and freely. I doubted that by the end of the course, I'd feel confident enough to step off without thinking of every possible way I could die. My brain just didn't work that way, or allow me to relax. But, at least this time, I knew what I was expecting when I would let myself fall. I saw Turner reach the bottom and give a thumbs up. Guess it was my turn. Getting clipped in, I lowered myself to a seated position and allowed gravity to do its job. No running starts for me.

I heard Turner say a little "whoop" for me when I was near the platform. When I got to him, I was successfully stopped by Joe, and unclipped.

"You're getting good at this," Turner commended.

I rolled my eyes. "Did I really have a choice? Seems to be the only way down at this point."

"You have a point."

"If I go on another date with you, I swear I'm going to need in writing and possibly a blood fingerprint what you're plans are. No more of this surprise freaking Annabelle out stuff."

He laughed. "But you're doing it aren't you? Are you enjoying it?"

I thought for a moment. "I think I'll find it enjoyable *after* I get home and realize I'm safe and sound from your crazy antics."

"Oh, Annabelle, these aren't crazy antics. Unless I take you skydiving or bungee jumping, this is quite tame."

My eyes got round. "I will never throw myself out of a perfectly good airplane for shits and giggles, Turner Brooks. So count me out."

"Noted."

He was amused by me. Joe was standing back allowing our moment and not interrupting our date. I kind of wished he would keep us moving so we could get this over with. Wait a second . . . this was the third platform. Didn't Serenity say this was the one that would be interesting? *Crap.* I looked around for anything that was different about this one versus the last two. That's when I saw it. There was a small wooden bridge that extended outwards about six feet. A cable went across it but it looked just like the ones we'd just traveled on. Maybe we were supposed to walk out and step off. Why in the world would we do that instead of doing it from right here? The bridge looked unsteady.

"Are we going?" I asked, ready to keep moving.

Joe came into my line of sight. "Yep, but here's where you have two options. You can either go down this one like you have the others, *or . . .*" his "or" sounded ominous. "You can walk out on this little plank here like a pirate, and take a leap of faith."

Turner wagged his eye brows at me. "Argh!" He tried to sound like a pirate.

"Not funny." I glared at him. "What do you mean a leap of faith? As in, just step off? Do you slide down the line still?"

Joe shook his head. "Nope. This one is a little simpler than that. You jump off the edge and once you're at the bottom, you walk to the next station."

I gulped. Were they insane? I already thought the was the worst idea ever was throwing myself over the edge of a hillside, but now they are asking me if I *want* to plummet eighty feet to the bottom? No way, no how. I already knew my answer. I was barely comfortable with this whole zip lining thing, this was just insanity to me. And of course I didn't need to ask Mr. Daredevil if he planned on jumping. He was.

"You going to do it?"

"Hell no. I'm quite fond of my legs and arms being intact, thank you very much."

Turner stepped into my little bubble again. Why does he do that? His woodsy aftershave washed over me and made me slightly dizzy. Men should not smell this good. He brushed his hand down from my shoulder to my elbow leaving a little trail of goose bumps in its path.

"It's not really the kind of free fall you're thinking it is. The line catches you and lowers you halfway down."

I met his blue eyes head on. "That halfway is still too far for me. I'll go the 'traditional' route." I gave air quotes.

"You're very stubborn, you know that?"

"Ha! So says the king of Stubborn Land."

Then he did something I didn't expect. He bent down and lightly kissed the tip of my nose. My poor heart went into over drive. Until now, Turner had yet to make any move to actually kiss me. Sure he'd kissed my hand at the end of our other date, but that didn't count. Not like this. And, of course, he chose now to plant a sweet delicate one on me when my nerves were already a hot mess. I'll give him credit though, it did shift my attention to other things. Like how tender he was. How in that split second I could tell his lips were silky soft. And now how I wanted to grab him by his collar and pull him down to me and kiss him the way I'd been thinking about for the past two weeks. I felt flushed all over and I shifted on my feet. Needing a little air, I cleared my throat.

"Well, you better make the plunge to your death. Your mom's number is in your phone right?"

He gave me another full bellied laugh. "Yes, it's in my phone." He started making his walk out on the very flimsy wooden boards. The further out he went the more it wobbled. "Annabelle?"

The sound of his voice calling my name felt like it was a shot straight to my soul. Why was I feeling this way?

"Yes?"

"There's more where that came from."

He leapt. My God, could the dude get any more brazen or cocky? Did it make my heart leap for joy? Yep. But that wasn't the point here. Clearly he thought he could do whatever he wanted if he sweet talked enough, or put me under his little spell and got close enough. No wonder all those women fell for him. He was like a little devil in scrubs. Err . . . well actually khaki shorts and a t-shirt that all fit him entirely too well. The bastard.

Looking over the edge, he landed on a black cushioned mat that was well worn from other jumpers.

"You proud of yourself?" I called down.

"Yes, ma'am. You really should try it. It's more fun than you think."

I gave him the "ok" hand sign. "I'm good."

Joe hooked me up to the traditional line and told me Serenity was waiting for me at the other end. Only difference between the last two times I'd gone, and this time, I noticed my nerves weren't in full effect like they had been. I zoomed down the line thinking of nothing but Turner and his adorable mouth. I questioned if I would allow him to kiss me again if he tried. And if he did, would it be on my nose again, or on the lips. I was getting wrapped up in the thought of him when my feet touched the bottom. Turner was climbing up a ladder on the side to meet up with me.

"Was it a good one?"

Okay, was he referring to the ride, or the kiss? Certainly not the kiss, it was just on my nose.

"It was enjoyable."

He smiled. He knew I was questioning what his he was really asking. I rolled my eyes.

We spent the rest of the morning bantering back and forth, with quite a bit of heavy flirting. We exchanged information about one another that was completely meaningless and yet I found it interesting and fun. There was a bit more to Turner Brooks than I'd previously given him credit for. He more than intrigued me. When we were making the long drive back to my house, I'd come to the conclusion that I may actually *like* him. Sure it made me uncomfortable, but that was merely because I hadn't allowed myself to like or crush on anyone in years. Never saw the sense in it. But today, I opened myself up to the possibility of actually seeing where this could go. Granted, not if it meant putting my life at risk every time. But still, I liked him.

Once we made it to my door step, Turner looked down at me with wonder in his eyes.

"I want to go out with you again, Annabelle."

I laughed. "Why do you look like it amazes you that you're even asking me?"

His smile wowed me like it always did this close up. He was so beautiful it nearly knocked me off my feet.

"Because it does."

"You're an odd one, you know that?"

"Well, I could say the same about you. So what do you say? Another date?"

I tried to make him wait for an answer, I really did. But my answer came out faster than I planned.

"I'd love too. But wait . . ." I held up my finger. "I refuse to go anywhere that makes me jump off things, go faster than seventy miles per hour, or anything in general that I have to sign a paper stating I may die."

He snickered. "It'll be low key."

I turned my head slightly to the side showing him I was skeptical. "Okay, sir. Well, be careful heading back home. And again, thank you for today."

It got quiet. Like tense quiet. I was looking at him and he was looking at me. There was a moment in time where you knew he was going to kiss you, and you just had to be ready for it. I wasn't ready, but I'd take it. Turner bent at the waist. I went up on my tippy toes. Just when I thought our mouths were going to meet, he went left, and I felt his warm lips on my cheek. *My cheek?* Squeezing my hand and releasing it, he stood at his full height and wished me a good day. When he was gone, I went to sit on my back porch to ponder the whole date. I was really starting to get a complex. Turner had kissed me three different times now and not a single one of them was on the mouth. Not a single one of them was full of the passion or ferocity that I pictured him giving the other women he pushed into the supply closets at work. Was he even in to me? Was I his type? Maybe he was looking at me like a buddy, or someone cool to hang out with. I never got the friendship vibe from him, so was I reading him wrong? Maybe. That kind of stung a little. I guess the next date we had I would have to try and pick up on his cues a little more. I didn't want to invest too much more of myself in him if I was only friend material.

I waited for him to call and tell me what we were doing next.

CHAPTER SEVEN

Annabelle

IT WAS BEFORE MY FIRST twelve hour shift of the week and I decided to do something unplanned. I decided to stop in the NICU to check on the baby boy I'd helped deliver last week to see how he was doing. I hadn't ever been in here other than to do a few hours of clinicals. A few monitors were beeping and I was looking around the room at all the incubators and infants fighting for their lives. I viewed this room like I did the Oncology floor. People fighting for their lives wasn't my cup of tea. I was better off bringing lives into the world and sending them on their merry way. Not pushing them to take their next breath and watch the families cry or grieve over loss. I'd seen enough of that to last me a lifetime.

"Can I help you?" A tall blonde nurse approached me. She had gentle eyes and a soft voice.

"Um, yeah I was actually looking for a baby that I helped deliver last week that was brought down here." Crap, I didn't know his name. "He was unnamed when he left L&D, but the mother was an addict." I wracked my brain for her name. "Adalyn March." It occurred to me. "So it would be Baby March."

Her tone became even softer. "Oh yes, he's right over here." She led me to a far corner of the room. "He's quite the little fighter."

As we approached, a baby small enough to fit in one of my hands was lying on his stomach, monitors attached to his frail body covered by almost transparent skin, a feeding tube in his nose that likely went directly to his stomach, and a breathing tube. It was almost painful to see. Such a small life fighting with everything he had, when he didn't deserve to be brought into this already cruel world in such a harsh manner.

"Has his mom come to see him?"

She looked perplexed. "Unfortunately, Baby March was abandoned. The day she delivered and was put in a post-partum room, she walked out a few hours later and hasn't been back. Nobody knows any contact information, and she never asked any questions about him before she left."

My hand automatically went up to my mouth. I felt like I wanted to be sick. How could a mother carry an infant, give birth, and just abandon it? Doesn't matter that she didn't carry him to term. He was her child. He would have loved her unconditionally and expected nothing in return other than what she could offer him. I just couldn't understand it.

The nurse, whom I'd learned was named Cassie, told me the baby's stats and what the doctor was expecting from him over the next couple of days. When babies came down here to NICU, they were usually checked in on every hour. They were given short term goals because that's what the staff had to rely on. Baby steps, if you will. Anything past that was just asking for too much too soon.

SLIDER

Cassie left me standing by Baby March's bed, and I turned to face him. He really was very fragile. I couldn't help what I was doing though. I stood there, and counted all ten fingers and all ten toes. Someone needed to do it for him. He deserved that much. I closed my eyes as tears welled in them. I took a deep breath and exhaled. Life wasn't fair. My parents were taken from me far too early, and I've been fighting to survive on my own for years. It was a struggle for me at sixteen. Why does an infant that weighed no more than three pounds have to suffer? Why was God picking him to have this battle? There were just some things I don't think I'd ever understand.

There was two covered holes in the incubator where nurses were able to reach gloved hands inside and make adjustments to his wires and tubes. Without asking, I went to the sink, washed my hands, and suited myself up to handle him. When I touched him for the first time, a small spark hit me. Not like electricity, but something indescribable. I wanted this baby to live. I *cared* that he was being cared for by the best. And I also realized, in that moment while my covered hand stroked his little back, that no matter how many nurses and doctors were checking in on him, I would be down here as often as possible ensuring that he knew he was loved. I stayed there with him for almost an hour, nurses moving around me, some even coming over to chat. They appreciated the extra support I was providing. But really, I was being selfish. I was doing this for me too. Something deep down inside of my very being *needed* the reassurance. He would be okay. I would accept nothing less.

It had been a very long day. I was on a quick ten minute break and on the tail end of my twelve hour shift. Visiting the baby this morning took a lot out of me emotionally, and assisting four other deliveries today was about all I could handle. I just wanted to stuff my face, and clock out. No wine or book necessary tonight. I simply needed sleep.

I was sitting in the locker/break room when the door opened and a little surprise walked in. Turner was carrying two Styrofoam boxes with something that smelled absolutely delicious. My poor stomach caught a whiff of the food too, and after that it was all over with. Was there an equally delicious man holding those boxes? No clue. Standing up I went straight to them with a one track mind. Turner held a box up, offering it to me. Snagging them from his hands, he chuckled.

"Hungry?"

I sat down and opened the lids. Deep fried chicken, mashed potatoes smothered in gravy, and coleslaw all attacked my senses. I think I moaned. Turner shifted in his chair. I glanced up at him and he watched me with an equally ravenous look I had for the chicken. I gulped.

"I'm sorry, did you ask me something?"

He cleared his throat. "Uh, yeah. I take it you're hungry?"

I picked up a leg and stuffed it in my mouth. I had no patience for politeness right now. "Mhmm. I've not eaten since six o'clock this morning."

He glanced down at his watch. "That was over thirteen hours ago. Don't they give you breaks on this floor?"

I swallowed a massive bite of piping hot, greasy chicken. "Yeah, but I have had too much other stuff to do. Charting, sending stuff down to the lab, giving the doctors updates. It's been quite the day."

"Sounds like it." His eyes roamed over my face. As the food was settling in my empty stomach, I was able to focus on something other than my hunger. I wasn't sure how I felt about him looking at me like that. "Y'all always this busy?"

I picked up a plastic fork and stuck it in the potatoes. "Not always. Just during shift changes it gets hectic, and of course if there's a full moon."

"I thought that was an old wives tale?"

I shook my head. "Didn't you learn this stuff during your OB rotation?" I couldn't help the laugh that came out.

"I don't think I paid much attention, honestly."

I explained, "It's not really an old wives tale. There's some truth to it. When there's a full moon, there's something to do with the gravity and earths pull and tilt that causes something to happen in a woman's body if she's close to her due date. It can help move along labor or get it started. I've checked out the calendar a couple times when there's one going on. The rooms tend to be a little fuller."

He thought it over. "Huh, I guess you learn something new every day."

I nodded. "Yes, I suppose you do."

I continued to eat my food in silence while Turner watched on. The other box of food remained untouched.

I pointed my fork in its direction. "Aren't you going to eat?"

"Yeah, I was just distracted by the view." He reached forward and pulled the white container toward him. He had the same thing I was eating. Picking up a thigh, he brought it to his mouth and took a bite. I watched his jaw and lips moving with rapt attention. I had no idea eating could be so sexy. "You okay over there?"

The smugness in his tone told me he knew exactly what he was doing to me. *Damn it, Annabelle, get your shit together. This wasn't the time or the place.*

"I'm fine. So anyway, what made you come to my little neck of the woods? And how did you know I was even here?"

"I called your charge nurse."

"That's a little stalkerish don't you think?"

"Not when I had intentions of bringing you dinner and we could talk about our next date."

"Still don't know how I feel about that."

He raised one perfect brow. "The date, or that I made the call."

"Both."

"Well . . . too bad."

Cocky bastard. "So what about this date? Weren't you supposed to call me or something?"

Turner shrugged his wide shoulders. "I could have, but I decided this was much more fun."

I think I ate to fast. I was already full and I'd barely finish a leg and a couple bites of potato. I sighed. "If watching me stuff my face like stoned college kid is fun for you, you should see me when I'm home alone and have a box of chocolates. Definitely disgusting."

He was amused. "Noted."

I waved my fork in the air. "No, sir. I was making a statement. It's not something you'll actually ever see."

"If you say so. Now, about this date."

"I'm listening."

Two nurses from my floor walked in. One of which was little Miss Red Silk herself. She paused in the doorway when she saw Turner sitting with me and her mouth dropped open. He barely flashed a glance in their direction. Did he not recognize her or was she that forgettable? By the look on her face, I'd say she was definitely offended by his lack of attention. I wanted to roll my eyes, but what prevented me from doing it was Turner refusing to care that someone else was around and could hear us. The slutty nurse, Robin, whom I rarely worked with anymore because she started doing on-call hours, grabbed whatever it was she was after out of her locker and slammed it shut. I can't say I wouldn't behave the same way she did if I was shunned so easily. When she stormed out of the room, I had to bite the inside of my cheek. No, I didn't feel egotistical that I was currently the girl Turner was paying attention to. But he did have a way of making you feel special.

"Annabelle, eyes right here please." His voice was deep and demanding. That pull I'd felt toward him since the first time we'd met was very evident and reeling me right in.

It was not fair that someone could have that color eyes and be so mesmerizing. I'd love to take him to the tropics just to see if they really were the same color as the ocean.

"I'm listening."

"Hmmm, if you say so. This weekend my parents asked if we all wanted to come over for dinner. Something about my mom missing her boys, blah blah blah. Anyway, I know both of my parents enjoyed your company, and frankly so do I. So would you like to join me?"

My head jerked back. "Why does this feel like a 'meet the family' sort of date?"

His brow furrowed. "Definitely not. And could you even count it as that when you've already met them?"

He made a point. "Touché."

"Oh, and if you come, you'll have to bring tennis shoes this time."

"Why's that?"

"Baseball, Annabelle. We play baseball every time we get together."

Oh, yes, I wasn't even thinking about their family traditions. "Well, I work on Saturday 'til six. Sometimes it's a little later depending on the number of laboring mothers and deliveries."

"That's not a problem. They will be barbequing so I'm sure dinner will be later than normal. Dad's a bit meticulous on the grill."

I had no reason to refuse. It wasn't like he was taking me on some wild ride again. Plus, my friends would be there to act as my comfort. How intimate could Turner and I get with his family around?

"Alright, you have yourself a date." Seemed low key enough.

Standing up from the table, he pushed his chair back. "You done with your food?"

I nodded.

He tossed them in the trash as he made his way to the door. "See you in a couple days, Beautiful."

My stomach flip flopped. He didn't even stick around after making me all mushy, he just walked out. I smiled to myself. Well, looks like I'd be seeing if I could keep myself safe and uninjured. Ironic that he's taken me on two dates now that I could have easily hurt myself, and yet the one place I was heading this weekend is where I managed to end up on my ass. Guess it's challenge accepted, Annabelle.

CHAPTER EIGHT

Annabelle

I WANTED TO FIND TIME to check on Baby March before I had to leave for the Brooks' house, but unfortunately it was already past six, and I still had another thirty minute drive ahead of me. Turner was going to wait for me, but I insisted that he go ahead of me. I didn't want his family to hold off on dinner just because I was running late. I even suggested taking a rain check but he assured me it was fine.

"Hey, I'm heading out. All my patients have been passed off. Have a good weekend," I called over my shoulder to my charge nurse.

"You too, hon," she replied.

Once out in the parking garage, I climbed into my car, tossed my bag onto the passenger seat and got on the road. I was actually looking forward to this evening. I may have been more nervous if this was my first time meeting the Brooks family, but it wasn't. Being around this family was comforting. I wasn't sure if that was odd, but I accepted the emotion. Paul and Donna had a way of making you feel like you were one of their kids. I'd be willing to bet they never met a stranger. Rolling the windows down, and turning the radio up, I sat back and enjoyed my short drive to their house.

SLIDER

Turner came outside to greet me when I pulled into the half circle driveway. He opened my door and bent down to greet me with a kiss on the cheek, I was motionless. Normally, I didn't get this from him until the end of the date. Apparently, he was trying to keep me on my toes by switching things up. I sighed deeply, unable to stop the girlyness from escaping my throat.

He smiled a dazzling, warm smile at me. "Glad you made it."

After I got out of the car, he shut the door behind me and we started walking toward the house. The driveway contained several other parked vehicles, two of which I recognized as Keegan and Macie's. I didn't think Macie would be here, but knowing Keegan she probably talked her into it.

"Me too."

"How was your shift?"

"Long and tedious. But when it comes to labor, sometimes tedious is good." I laughed. "Excitement on my floor means a momma is struggling or baby is. Not necessarily something we want." It was weird how comfortable this simple conversation was to have with him. Almost like we'd done it for years.

"Hmmm, I see what you're saying. Well, I hope you worked up an appetite. Pretty sure my dad bought every meat the market down the street had in the display case. Plus, my mom made her famous dill potato salad and caprese salad, and knowing her, there will be no less than three different desserts to choose from later. I think Keegan brought some food, too."

My stomach rumbled. "Oh, I definitely have an appetite right now. Maybe too much of one."

He squeezed my hand and winked at me. That rumble turned to flutters. He was getting to me.

"Well, eat your fill. Regardless, I know Mom will send you home with a container full of leftovers. That's half the reason I come over."

I slapped at his arm and smiled. "You're such a guy. Does your mother know you use her for her cooking?"

"Absolutely. My brothers and I have been eating them out of house and home since we were kids. She lives for this."

I'm pretty sure she probably did. In the short time I'd known Donna, I got the impression she was your typical southern woman and mom. Small wasn't in her vocabulary unless it referred to herself. Her home was immaculate, her cooking was perfection, she raised her boys to be southern gentlemen, and she did it all without a hair out of place on her head.

Stepping into the front door, I was greeted by so many smells, the scent of comfort food permeating throughout the home. It has been a while since I'd walked into something like this. In fact the last time was when I was here.

"Hi, Annabelle! How are you, honey?" Donna came around the corner dressed in a cute summer maxi dress and an apron. Sweetness poured out of her voice.

My automatic reaction was to go to her. She opened her arms to me and greeted me with a hug. I was *not* an affectionate person, but for whatever reason with her, it felt natural and okay. Donna even smelled good. Like a mom, if that made any sense.

113

"I'm good." I released from her embrace. "Thank you so much for having me. I'm sorry I'm late."

She waved her hand in front of me. "Oh please. You're not late, you're right on time. Paul is just finishing up on the grill and Keegan is getting everyone's drinks. Come on in and make yourself at home. What would you like to drink with dinner? We have lemonade, sweet tea, or I think there's some beer in the fridge downstairs, Turner could go get you one."

I looked up at him. He was beaming down at his mom. Huh, I never noticed it before, but he was definitely a momma's boy. It was written all over his face. The adoration in his eyes couldn't be missed.

"Actually, a lemonade would be fine, thank you," I replied politely.

"You got it." She winked at me. Her smile and Turner's were exactly the same. My eyes fixated on her straight teeth and dazzling expression. "Son, fix her a glass please, and go check on your daddy. I'm worried he's going to burn the chicken breasts attempting to get those darn char lines perfect."

Turner sighed. "Yes, ma'am."

"Without the sass, young man," she admonished.

I had to bite the inside of my cheek to keep from laughing at their exchange.

"Yes, ma'am."

"I'll be right back." He squeezed my hand again, and released it. When he walked out of the foyer, I gave Donna my attention again. She was standing with her hands on her hips, shaking her head.

"He was never my stubborn one, but, boy, he liked to push my buttons."

"Turner, not stubborn?" Now I did laugh.

"Has he been giving you a hard time?"

I thought back to previous conversations, and places he'd taken me. "Oh, you could say that."

"Sounds like my boy could use a talkin' to."

I reached forward and touched her arm. "No, it's fine. I'm teasing. I've just learned he doesn't like to take no for an answer." I realized what I said after the words already left my mouth, but thankfully Donna didn't reply to my comment the way it could have been taken.

"No, he doesn't," she agreed.

"It's not always a bad thing though. He's been . . . sweet."

She exhaled. "That's good. Well, I'm going to go check on the pies. Keegan and Macie are in the dining room if you want to go say hello."

"Do you need any help in the kitchen?" Not that I'd be much help. I'd never been much of a baker or chef.

"No, but thank you."

I nodded and headed to the dining room. The house was big, but I remembered where some of the rooms were from the wedding and my last visit. I heard Macie's loud voice echoing across the way, which told me I was heading in the right direction. Once around the corner, I saw Keegan placing napkins and silverware next to each plate, and Macie sitting with her arms crossed. She looked like she was pouting.

"Hey, beautiful girl." Keegan glanced up at me.

"Hey, girls."

"Ugh, another one that has fallen for the Brooks' Charm." The distaste in Macie's voice was strong.

I gave her a perplexed look. "What are you talking about? I'm confused."

She rolled her eyes. "Turner. That's what I'm talking about."

I looked to Keegan for some clarification.

"Mace, stop it. Don't mind her. She's extra pissy today for some reason. Is it getting close to your time of the month?"

"Shark week? Pssh, no. I'm just realizing I'm surrounded by suckers."

"Okay, now that's enough. Whatever this bad mood you're in is, cut it out. You're going to ruin my good time, Annabelle's, and the rest of the family," Keegan snapped.

"Hey." Macie raised her hands in the air. "I'm just making an observation."

"You're also making an ass out of yourself."

Macie jerked her head back. I needed to step in before this escalated further.

"Alright, ladies, simmer down. I don't know what's going on, but whatever it is, it's not worth it."

"You have no idea," Macie mumbled.

"I guess not, but Keegan has a point. I don't know what you're feeling sour about, but maybe we can talk about it after dinner, and we've all had something good to eat. Okay?'

She tipped her head down, clearly frustrated. Keegan shook her head and kept setting the table. Never had I seen these two girls fight, but something was bothering both of them. I wasn't one to be a mediator, but I would be right now if I had to be. It stayed silent for a couple of minutes before Turner came into the room smelling of the grill outside. He took one look at me and came to my side.

"You okay?" he asked quietly. His eyes roamed over to the other girls.

"Yeah."

He brushed my hair back behind my ear in a tender way. His fingers gently caressed the side of my cheek. All thoughts of Keegan and Macie left my mind. I was standing there front of Turner and as far as I was concerned, nobody else was in the room. How did he have the power to do that?

"You sure?"

"Mhmm."

He caught onto the trance he was putting me in and must've decided it wasn't the time or the place. Stepping back, he greeted the two girls. Both mumbled hellos.

Donna came into the room and clapped her hands, completely oblivious to the tension between everyone.

"Alright, who's hungry?"

As if by magic, all of us shifted and the room lightened significantly. Hmmm, and I thought Turner was capable of some crazy shit. Turner pointed me in the direction of where we were sitting, and everyone filed in over the next couple of minutes. It didn't take long before we were all seated and our plates were filled. Chatter of work, new dogs, and college were amongst the conversation. If there was any rigidness remaining, it was only between Macie and Dodger, who were sitting on opposite ends of the table from each other. Clearly this was where her issue laid. I didn't understand it and I wasn't sure I ever would. Dodger was head over heels for Macie, and whether she realized it or not, she felt the same way. Never in my life have I seen two people more meant for each other, and yet fight against it so hard. I didn't know who was pushing who away, but I did know it wasted precious time. If there's one thing I've learned from my parents, it's that time is invaluable. I'd give anything to have another five minutes with them.

We all were sitting back in our chairs, nursing overstuffed bellies when Keegan asked me a question.

"Lauren, from NICU, said you've been visiting a baby you helped deliver. How's he doing?"

The question seemed innocent, but it made me pause in my response. It wasn't like I was trying to slip in and out unnoticed, but obviously I was going in there often enough to cause some talk.

I felt Turner's eyes on the side of my face, but I ignored it. "He's doing well. They just lowered his oxygen and he isn't struggling, so that's good."

"What baby are we talking about?" Donna chimed in.

Ugh, way to go Keegan. This wasn't a subject I wanted to talk about. Especially with all these people, let alone Turner listening. I knew as soon as we were alone, he was going to ask me questions. He was reading me right now.

I glanced around the table and all eyes were on me. "I had a patient a couple weeks ago give birth to a premature baby. I sometimes go check on it."

Donna's eyes softened. "Oh my, that's very sweet of you."

"Well, it wasn't quite that simple. The mom was an addict. She ended up abandoning him the same day she gave birth. Seriously, it was terrible. I'm telling you, had I been the delivering nurse that day, I would have given her a piece of my mind." Keegan was getting riled up. I wanted to slap her for divulging so much.

"When was this?" Turner asked.

I didn't give him my eyes. I didn't want to. He'd see exactly what talking about the baby did to me.

"It was the day after the wedding."

"I don't know how a mother could just leave their baby like that." Donna had tears in her eyes. God, this subject needed to be changed quick. "It was a boy?"

I nodded.

"Do you know what's going to happen to him when he's strong enough to get out of the hospital?"

This was a question that plagued me more and more as the baby grew stronger. I honestly didn't know what would happen to him, but I could only assume he would go into the state's care.

"I'm not certain. But there are a lot of adoptive parents out there that would love to have a newborn baby. Just don't know what kind of long term effects he will have from everything his mother was on. So it could be a tricky case."

Turner touched the small of my back. He was giving me comfort when I didn't even realize I needed it.

"So, yeah, great dinner time convo," Macie piped in, clearly not wanting to talk about this any longer. Thank God, I could hug her. "Donna, I'm going to start cleaning up, is that okay?"

All of the attention that was on me, shifted to her.

"Sure, darlin'. I'll help."

119

Macie shook her head. "No, it's okay, I don't mind. You made a fabulous dinner, you deserve to relax and enjoy your boys." She stood up and grabbed the plates nearest to her. When she walked out, Dodger stood up and followed. I knew I wasn't the only one that would like to know what was going on with those two.

"So, are we having dessert first or are we heading out to the field?" Wrigley asked, stretching his arms above his head.

"I vote field," Paul said.

"I second that," Camden replied. "What do you want to do. babe?"

Keegan put her hand on his. "I'm fine either way."

Paul rubbed his hands together. "Looks like it's game time."

We all got up from the table and made our way to the garage.

The guys packed everything up, and Keegan went back into the house to get Macie and Dodger. Turner led me to one of the golf carts and sat down next to me.

"You going to play on my team?"

I raised my brow. "I don't know. Are you any good?"

"You've seen me play before, Annabelle."

"I wasn't paying that close attention."

He rubbed his chest with his fist. "Ouch! My ego has been struck."

I playfully shoved him. "No, it hasn't, hush."

"And here I thought you were staring at me the whole time."

I leaned in close to him. His eyes watched me like a hawk. "I'll let you in on a little secret, though." I spoke even quieter,

"I did watch you during dinner." I winked and faced forward, hoping we would leave soon.

Keegan stepped outside looking frustrated and ready to hit something. "Macie isn't coming. She said she isn't feeling well and is going home."

Donna started to get off the golf cart. "Does she need someone to take her home?"

"Dodger is telling her he'd take her, but you know her. She's fighting him tooth and nail and is refusing to be near him."

Speaking of, Dodger came out of the house, slamming the door behind him. He ignored all he looks we were throwing his way, grabbed a bat bag, and walked out of the garage without a word.

"Well, alright," Turner said. "Looks like trouble in Love Land."

"Stop it," I scolded.

"I'm sure if Macie needs something she will let someone know." Paul redirected the family's attention. "Let's head over."

Nothing more needed to be said. The patriarch of the family spoke and that was the end of it. We all took off in our carts and drove down the road to the empty baseball field the family owned and was very familiar with. I'd only been out here one time, but that one time was all it took. I felt comfortable, like this was something I'd done regularly with them. I couldn't pinpoint why this family was so welcoming and warm. They all had that way about them that invited you in, made you feel at ease. I doubt they ever met a stranger, and a stranger never felt out of place with them. It must be their gift.

Unloading everything, Dodger was standing in front of a fence, throwing a baseball as hard as he could. It bounced back and he'd catch it with his bare hands. Clearly, he was letting off some steam. He didn't even turn to look at us when we rolled up.

"Teams," Wrigley said rubbing his hands together. "Me, Mom, Camden, and Annabelle."

"What? No way, she's on my team asshole,." Turner retorted.

"Dad, Turner, Keegan, and Dodger." He nodded, proud of himself and ignoring his brother.

"No, teams need to be broken up differently. We will take Annabelle, y'all can have Dodger."

"Don't be crazy, big brother. You know I gave you the better team."

"Hey," Camden piped in. "Need I remind you who was picked up by the number one college in the nation?"

"Dude, you say that every time we come out here. We know . . . it's old news," Wrigley grumbled.

I got the distinct impression it was a sore spot for him. Wonder if it was some friendly brotherly competition.

"We good with the teams?" Paul said, stepping between the brothers.

Both boys nodded.

It was determined that I was with Turner, which I was somewhat disappointed about. I wanted to test my abilities at kicking his ass, but couldn't very well do that when we were both trying to score a run. We played the game, having five innings. There was so much laugher and banter. Best part, I managed to stay on two feet this time. Couldn't say as much for Paul. He felt it was necessary to slide into third base, effectively taking out his youngest, and giving poor Donna a heart attack in the process. She yelled at him while checking out his ripped pants, saying he wasn't twenty years old anymore and couldn't play rough or someone was going to get hurt. You know, typical mom stuff.

Donna ended up sitting out after Paul's little spill. It frazzled her. When I stood off to the side waiting for my turn to bat, she came over to me.

"So sad about the baby."

I glanced down at her. Oh God, did we have to talk about this again?

"Yes, it is."

"Are you okay?"

I tilted my head to the side. "Yes. Why?"

She gave me a gentle smile. "Because, honey, I read people. No, not like that psychic crap you see on TV. But I can sense when someone is holding back and not letting their feelings through. Kind of like Macie and Dodger. I know those two, and I know how much she loves him. She has her issues she is sorting through and they will eventually come together. And when we were sitting at dinner, I saw your hands twisting together and your eyes got glassy." She paused and let me take in what she was saying. "That baby means something to you."

I gulped. "Sure I care about him. He's an innocent child."

I wasn't fooling her. "It's more than that. I'm not sure what your connection is with him, but I will tell you this, keep going to him. Visit him, hold him, feed him, let him feel loved. Love is what heals. We don't know what God has in store for that little man, but you're a kind and sweet person to go to him and care for him like you have. That tells me something about your heart and what kind of woman you are. I have no doubt your momma is looking down on you and is proud of you."

Okay and cue the tears. Who the hell is Donna Brooks and where in the world did she come from? This wasn't anything I wanted to hear right now. I was not a religious person and I had no clue if my parents were in heaven seeing and watching everything I did in life. I didn't think they were anywhere. When they died, they died. I didn't know if there was a God, so I couldn't believe in the saying, "he had a plan for them." Taking away a young girl's family was not a plan. It was awful, and painful. Cruel. It ripped my soul out and shredded it. My parents were in the ground forty minutes from this baseball field and that's what I actually believed.

I didn't want to be rude to a woman who's been nothing but kind to me, so I mustered a smile.

"Thank you."

She patted my shoulder. "You're welcome. Now, if my youngest boy could find a good girl, like you three, I'd be a happy momma."

I was perplexed. "What?"

She waved her hand in the air. "That Wrigley is a thorn in my heel. I love him more than pie, but that boy is so lax about life, I don't know if he will ever settle down. I knew my other three would, but him . . . well, I'll fall off my rocker the day he brings home a girl and says she's a keeper." She chortled like she just told the best joke.

I was still caught up in the previous conversation when she threw another glass of water in my face. She spoke like Turner was settling down. No. No way, was it with me. I was only just beginning to relax with him and let him in. Could we at least have our first kiss before we started talking forever or settling down?

"Oh, your turn, honey!" Donna called my attention back to the game.

Right. Who the hell could hit a ball after all that mess?

I did okay ,for the most part, the rest of the game, but I knew Donna watched me. I realized just how much she watched *everyone*. This was how she knew things. She was an observant little thing.

Game time was over and time to wrap everything up after playing two more innings. It was dark outside, but a couple lights kept the field fairly lit. Mosquitos were getting a tad ridiculous and Keegan said they needed to go home to check on the dog. I was ready to go home to my cat and glass of wine. I felt dead on my feet.

"Hey, you," Turner said to me.

"Hmmm?"

"Walk with me." He took my hand and held me back.

The family cleared the field and drove back to the house.

"Did you have a good time?" he asked.

Besides discussing a couple subjects that I would have rather had my wisdom teeth removed again than talk about, I can't say I didn't.

"Yes. Your mom is quite the cook."

"She is. She holds the records for the best Blackberry Pie and shrimp creole in three counties."

I laughed. "Oh God, don't talk about food. After playing the game, I'm ready for another full meal."

He poked my side. "You could stand to gain a bit."

I stopped walking. "Uh, no, sir. I've been eating anything I can get my hands on because of my crazy schedule at the hospital. Tonight is the first time I've had a homemade meal in over a month. Take out is all I have time for. And I certainly haven't been hitting the gym."

He gave my hand a tug, pulling me into him. The hardness of his chest made me breathe heavier. My other hand came up on its own accord and rested right over his heart. It was beating normally. Clearly, I didn't affect him like he was affecting me. If someone took my blood pressure right now it would be sky high and they'd cart me off to the hospital.

"You're kidding me, right?" he genuinely asked.

"Kidding you about what?"

"Your weight."

I tried to laugh it off. "No. I mean, I'm mostly teasing, but it wouldn't hurt for me to hit a gym every now and then so I can keep up with all the calories and chocolate cake . . . or pie, I've been eating."

He wanted to smile at that one, I know he did, but he remained serious.

"You're beautiful in every way, Annabelle. Sure your looks drew me in, but I've gotten to know you, and that heart of yours is huge. Gym or no gym, weight gain or no weight gain, you're still the same person to me."

I blinked rapidly. "You don't really even know me."

He leaned his head forward so his bright blue eyes were in a direct path with mine. "Oh, yes, I do. You may not share some parts of your life with me yet, but you will. In time, you will. And no matter what, it *still* doesn't change how loving and beautiful you are in the parts that you have shown me."

I was pulled back into that place that he was so good at putting me. A place where only Turner and I existed and I couldn't even feel if my own feet were touching the ground. I was floating, and all I thought about was if I wished hard enough for him to kiss me, he just might do it.

"Those are some pretty strong words, Dr. Brooks," I squeaked out.

He nodded. "Yes, they are."

I had no clue how close we were to the house, how far we had walked, if the crickets were still chirping or if they were waiting for the same thing I was waiting for. But it was happening. Turner released my hand and placed both of his on either side of my face. One of his thumbs brushed my cheek so tenderly that I barely felt it whisper across my skin. Nope, definitely no gravity on planet earth right now. As he came toward me, I did the only thing I could do. I closed my eyes and gave in to the power of him, and I let him lead the way.

His lips were a soft brush over mine at first. Like stepping your foot into open water and seeing if it was going to be warm or cold. Warmth was all I felt. My heart fluttered, then came crashing to a halt when he came back and applied more pressure this time, allowing me to really feel the sensation of his mouth pushing against mine. Tentatively, I opened, barely enough to suggest I wanted more. He took my suggestion and ran away with it. Turner Brooks wrapped one arm around my lower back, pulling me flush to him, and his other threaded into my hair. His tongue danced along the outside of my lips before plunging into my mouth demanding more. I sighed and melted into him. This kiss was unlike those crazy, inexperienced first kisses. There was no learning if one person liked it fast or slow, soft or hard, more tongue or lips. Turner was all of it. He was moving his mouth in a demanding manner, before he'd slow his pace and I'd follow suit. Never in my life had I been kissed like this. I didn't want it to end either. Not having any clue how long we stood like this, Turner kept the lead, but eventually ended the kiss with a tender peck, then sweetly kissed the tip of my nose.

My eyes were still closed when he said my name.

"Annabelle."

"Hmmm?"

"How are you feeling?"

How was I feeling? Did I even *have* any feeling? I wiggled my toes and dropped my arms from his chest. I had no clue I had gripped his shirt so tightly that the material was now wrinkled. Yeah, I had some feeling.

I bit my lip and shyly looked down. "I'm good."

He tipped my chin up with his index finger. "You sure?"

I wanted to bust out laughing. He knew what he had just done to me. I, Annabelle, had become unglued and allowed a man to make me feel something more than just a crush.

"Definitely sure."

He smirked. "Good. Let's walk."

We were still standing where he'd stopped me on the side of the road with no regard to neighbors seeing our public display of affection. Turner took my hand again, and started in the direction of the house. He made small talk about his family and how crazy they could be, while nothing wiped the perma-grin off my face. Was this what happiness felt like? Those ooey gooey girl feelings that the women in the hospital who fawned all over him gushed about? I didn't want to be one of them, but I felt it creeping in. I wanted to go home and tell Chaz all about the kiss like a teenage girl, while my fat cat looked on with disinterest. Indifference toward Turner was all but gone, and my need for more had replaced it. I walked beside him, wondering when he would ask me out again, and where it would be. I wanted to know if he would kiss me again, and if it would be just like this one. Things like relationships, dating, and love were not my forté. I didn't technically know how to take on any of it because I lacked experience. But I could see myself liking him more and more at this pace. He did all the right things, and he said all the right things. But history has shown me for over seven years that those things didn't necessarily add up to what was good for me. I didn't let people in for reasons I chose to keep to myself. I was going to have to seriously ask myself if it was time to let those walls down and see if life was going to play nice again. I couldn't afford to lose another person that I cared about without it destroying me. Pain was a feeling I was well acquainted with, but it was an emotion that given the chance to strike me down again, I knew I wouldn't survive it.

Turner and I ended our night on a good note. His mom sent me home with a container of food, and she slid a note on top of it with her phone number and a short message to contact her if I ever needed anything. Then in smaller letters she wrote:

PS. *What you're doing for the baby is admirable. If I can help, let me know.*

When I climbed into my car and read it, I wanted to crumple it up and throw it on the floor board. Only reason it didn't was because it tugged at my heart. I ended up putting the note in my purse where I could access it. I know I may have felt guarded while speaking to her, but intuition told me it was okay. I drove home with thoughts that I should let these people in because I knew they had my best interests at heart. I didn't want to spend the rest of my life keeping people on the outside. Turner was changing me, a piece at a time, but I was changing.

CHAPTER NINE
Turner

EVER SINCE THAT KISS, I've been thinking about more. I wanted Annabelle beneath me, feeling every inch of me as I pushed inside of her. It has been a constant thought since her mouth was on mine. The self-control I had to display that day to not press her against a parked vehicle and do what I'd been dying to do for months now was unreal. I don't think I've ever held back from taking what I wanted from a woman before. Not that any of them really held me back anyway. But my life was a revolving door of women. Never have I had to work for sex. Annabelle, isn't like that though. It has not been work. It's been *genuine*. The draw to her, the desire to have more than her physically, was a new emotion. Did this make me an asshole for being that way to the others? Probably. I've had feelings for a few of them, but they were never the kind where I wanted to bring someone home to meet my parents. Those women were fun, and kept me occupied when I got bored with my life. Okay, yeah, I was the world's biggest asshole for that. Nothing I could do about it now. 'Cause right now, one girl had my attention, and she's had it since the day she had lunch at my parent's house.

I was on call earlier this morning and had to come in to surgically correct someone's knee. I wasn't particularly busy at the moment, and I considered going up to Annabelle's floor to surprise her. Admittedly, I had already made a call to see if she was on duty. Sure, I could have asked her, but a surprise visit seemed more fun. Yeah, I wanted to see her. Getting on the elevator, I took it down one floor to Labor and Delivery. The nurse's station was unoccupied except for a young girl that I'd never seen before. She glanced up at me briefly, then looked back to her work, only to shoot her eyes back up to mine. Her whole demeanor screamed of inexperience. She was new and had no clue who I was. After this, based off her expression, I'd guess she'd learn.

"Can I help you with something, Doctor . . ." She looked at my name tag hanging from the pocket of my scrubs. "Brooks?"

Not that I wanted to butter her up, but I figured it wouldn't hurt to lay on some charm. Giving her a million dollar smile that seemed to work on majority of the ladies, I watched it affect her just as I suspected it would. She fluttered her eye lashes and smoothed her smock down even though there wasn't a wrinkle in sight.

"Actually, I was wondering if you could point me in the direction of where one of your nurses is right now."

"Oh, um, sure. Who are you looking for?"

"Annabelle. I was told she was on today."

Disappointment played over her face. "She is, but I think she's on her break. I can let her know that you stopped in if you'd like."

"No, that's okay. I just had some things to discuss with her, but it can wait."

If she wasn't readily available, I had no interest in keeping this conversation going. Again, I never said I wasn't the world's biggest asshole. Turning away, I made my way to their break room. She wasn't there. Huh. Where would she go? I could look in the cafeteria, but I had a feeling I wouldn't find her there. Then it hit me. I knew where she was. It was instinct. I had gotten better at reading her over the last couple months, and given the time to think about it, it should have been the first place I looked when they said she wasn't there.

I used my security card to go through the door of the NICU. I wasn't familiar with this area of the hospital at all, but it wasn't that hard to see everything. The room was open with babies in incubators spread throughout the space. I scanned the room for her strawberry blonde hair. Sure enough, there she was. In the back corner, Annabelle sat in a rocking chair, holding quite possibly the smallest baby I'd ever seen. I approached her slowly, like you would walking up on a lion, unsure if it will attack or allow you closer. The air around her screamed protective. She cradled the baby to her chest and if anybody would get too close she looked like she would pounce. I was only a few feet away from her and she still hadn't seen me. I observed her. She rocked back and forth, and soothingly rubbed his naked back. His fragile body swam in the too large diaper on his lower half, and her other hand held him under his bottom. A few wires kept him connected to the machines that monitored his oxygen levels and pulse. Annabelle whispered words to him that I couldn't hear. This wasn't what I expected to walk in to when I caught up with her.

When she spoke about the baby she helped deliver and she would check in on, I assumed she would peek in on him, ask the nurses what his progress was, and would leave. This wasn't what was happening at all. It was clear as day to me. This baby meant something to her. She felt for him. She was caring for him as if he were her own. My presence became known when she heard a nurse coming up beside me. When her aqua colored eyes met mine, I saw several emotions flash across her face—shock, uncertainty, anger, and embarrassment. I did my best to express understanding without words. I wasn't judging her. No, I didn't get what was going on here, but that didn't mean I wasn't empathetic and wouldn't try to understand.

"Turner." She said my name almost like a question.

I walked closer to where she was rocking 'til I was directly in front of her. "Hi."

"What are you doing here?"

"I went to your floor to surprise you, but you weren't there."

"How did you know I was here?"

"I didn't."

"I don't understand."

"It was a guess."

She watched me with a very calculated look upon her face. I could tell Annabelle had no idea what do to or say, but she was in defense mode. Instead of making a big deal out of seeing her like this, I decided it was best that I shift the subject and mood toward what I intended on asking her before I came down here.

"So I was thinking, dinner at my place might be a good idea."

"Your place?"

"Yes. I'm kind of a good cook. No worries though, nothing cheesy like candles and Marvin Gaye or anything. I'll still keep it simple, but I thought another easy and relaxing date would be nice while I think of something else to get you questioning why you say yes to me." I tossed a smile in her direction, hoping she'd enjoy the tease.

Even though she was holding such a small little person in her hands, her attention was on me and that adorable eyebrow went up. "Dinner at your place, because you're still thinking of other dates to take me on to make me question my life?"

"Well, that's one way of thinking of it."

"Doctor Brooks, you're not funny."

"Actually, I am."

"No, not really."

"I think I'm hysterical. But that doesn't answer my question."

"I don't believe you actually *asked* me a question."

Touché, sassy girl. I guess I didn't phrase it like a question. There she goes again, keeping me on my toes. "Would you like to come to my place this evening, so I may cook you dinner, and we could talk and drink wine?"

She cracked a smile at me. "I thought you said there would be no cheesiness?"

I put my hand up to my chest. "There was no cheese in that question."

She looked at me long and hard, her hand mindlessly patting the infant's back. "What time do you want me there?"

"Seven. We'll make it a late dinner."

"Text me your address and let me know what you need me to bring."

I winked at her. "Yes, ma'am." I took a step toward her and bent down. My lips met her forehead and I kissed her. "And we will be talking about this."

When I pulled away her eyes were huge on her face. I wasn't trying to scare her, but we'd gone out enough that I should be able to ask some questions and get answers. If she didn't want to tell me the depths of her feelings that was fine. She would eventually. I was ready for more from Annabelle. I wanted to pick her brain and learn how she ticked. I wanted her physically and in every way possible. I craved her like no other. Tonight, I would get from her what I wanted.

⋄ ⋄ ⋄ ⋄ ⋄

Annabelle

Never had I anticipated Turner coming to the NICU. Him seeing me like that was almost too much. Had I not been holding the baby, I probably would have gotten more upset than I let on. First his mom asking too many questions, now him. And what did he mean we would be talking about this? There was nothing to talk about. It wasn't any of his business, either. If he thought we were talking about anything relating to this, he was going to be disappointed.

I didn't have time to think about Turner during the last half of my shift. We had three moms arrive in active labor and all three delivered within an hour of each other. When I finished my portion of the paperwork, I clocked out and headed home. I had thought about when the time would come that I would be stepping foot in Turner's space, but I figured I would be more nervous than I currently was. I chalked it up to exhaustion. I was dead on my feet and his idea for wine and food sounded amazing to my tired brain and body right now.

When I got home, I changed into comfortable jeans, a loose tank top, and took my hair out of the ponytail it had been in all day. I pulled it half up, and let some pieces on the side fall around my face. There was no need for make-up but I did add a little bit of gloss to my lips before I got back into my car and made the drive to his place. Turns out he lived on the tenth floor of a building not far from the hospital. He had instructed me to pull into the parking garage and what number space to park in. When I got into the elevator the butterflies started their fluttering. I didn't know what I to expect from Turner tonight, but I was stepping foot into his space. It was his domain and his rules. Was tonight going to turn into something more than just a kiss? Would I allow it? I decided before I raised my hand to knock on the door, that I would just let things flow and see where the night took us. It went against the grain for me, however I couldn't deny that I wanted Turner Brooks. He intrigued me in every sense of the word. I desired him like no other, and at some point I needed to admit to myself that I honestly had no control with him. He held me captive when I got too close, and if he wanted something from me, I was going to let him take it.

I knocked softly. He opened the door and my mouth gaped. Wearing a pair of worn jeans, and a tight fitted t-shirt, not a single muscle wasn't on full display and open to my viewing. Even better, he was traipsing around without shoes or socks. He saw me checking him out and I made a show of closing my mouth and giving him a "fuck you, I may have been caught but it doesn't matter" smirk.

"Evening, Annabelle." He stepped to the side allowing me to come in.

"Doctor Brooks." I regarded him formally.

He shook his head as I walked past. Our banter and flirting was already starting and the evening was young. Following behind me, he closed the door and allowed me to scan my surroundings. It was a very modern, chic apartment, and exactly what I expected from him. Clean lines, black leather furniture, and an open floor plan. There was no true entry way into the space. I walked right into the living room where a large couch sat at an angle over the top of a gray area rug. A massive television covered a portion of the wall, and a very nice surround sound system hung in every corner that I could see. To the right was a kitchen that had gray cabinets and a black granite countertop. Stainless steel appliances rounded off the modern kitchen. It smelled amazing in here—an aroma of fresh herbs and spices with a touch of garlic. Stepping toward the kitchen, I saw the two wine glasses and a bottle of white and red wine next to them. Something was simmering on the stovetop, and two plates sat beside it.

I turned to look at him. "What's for dinner?"

"Chicken piccata over linguine, and garlic bread is in the oven." He skirted past me, barely brushing my bare arm. I shivered. "I wasn't sure if you liked red or white, but reds usually go better with Italian."

"Red is fine," I concurred.

He poured me half a glass, while he did the same for himself. "Feel free to relax and make yourself at home. There are stools on the other side of the bar if you care to sit there."

I did as he suggested. He went to the stove and stirred what was cooking. I took a seat on a silver stool that had no backing. It was slightly uncomfortable but for conversation sake, I'd stay here until it was time to eat.

"How was work?" he asked.

"Quite busy actually. Three deliveries."

"Were you in on all of them?"

"I was for two, the last I came in after baby was born and did some clean up."

"Do you ever get to go in during C-sections?"

"No, not really. I've seen a few, but there are other nurses on staff, that are trained for those."

Small talk, or genuine interest. Either way, the conversation flowed from one subject to another. I'd been there for about twenty minutes when he said the food was ready. He made my plate and carried it over to a black table. He stuck to his word. No candles were lit, and no weird music was being played. There was a clicker on the table near his chair and he picked it up and pushed a couple buttons. In a moment I heard Marvin Gaye's "Let's Get It On" start playing throughout the house.

I looked at him and raised a brow. "Really?"

He chuckled. "I'm totally teasing. Set that one up."

I laughed. "Well played."

He pushed another couple buttons and some low key country came on.

"I promise no more 'cheese.' But I had to tease."

I smirked. "Wasn't sure where you were going with that one."

He shook his head and dove into his food. I followed suit and silence ensued. It was still comfortable though. It felt like we'd done this many times before and it was natural to enjoy each other's company. Something I'd never felt with someone else before.

"You ever consider moving up to my floor?"

I paused with my fork midair. "I suppose I have."

"If a position opened up, would you consider it?"

I thought about it. "Maybe, but I'm enjoying where I'm at more than I expected too. The other nurses are quite nice and seeing the deliveries day in and day out, is very gratifying to me. No two births are the same, and it keeps me on my toes."

He pondered my words. Taking his last bite, he set his fork down and sat back in his chair. Blue eyes were staring me down and I swallowed my food almost whole. He had the ability to make me feel so comfortable one minute, and completely unglued the next. And could his shoulders be any wider?

"Chew your food a little better, Annabelle. I may know the Heimlich but that doesn't mean I want to perform it."

"Excuse me?"

"I see you." His voice got deeper.

"You see me?"

"Yes. I see everything."

Enough already. *Shake it off, Annabelle.* He was taking control and I needed it back. "Interesting." I broke eye contact and poked at my food. "So not only are you a comedian, we can add psycho stalker to your list of qualities. Noted."

He barked out a laugh. "And there you go again."

"What did I do?"

"I may see things about you, but one thing I can never figure out is what is going to come out of your mouth next. It keeps *me* on *my* toes."

"Glad I keep you entertained." I took his advice and chewed a little more thoughtfully.

He tilted his head to the side regarding me. I expected him to shoot back, but he didn't. Instead he stood, and picked up his plate and glass. "Finish up. I'm going to start the dishes and then we can sit and relax."

Relax. *Riiight*. Whatever that was with a man like him sitting next to me. Such a contradiction. I was able to feel at ease next to him, but also edgy. I only had a couple more bites to finish and I was stuffed. Like, certain my stomach was hanging over my pants and I'd be much more comfortable in yoga pants, stuffed. I'll give him credit, the man could cook. Certainly a quality his mom instilled. Mimicking what he'd done, I took my dishes over to him. I expected him to step out of the way so I could rinse mine off and put them in the dishwasher, but he took them from my hand instead.

"Thank you."

He eyed me curiously. "You're welcome. Go make yourself comfortable on the couch. I'll be over in a minute."

I did as he asked. Even though my heart was wanting to take a little galloping stroll in my chest, I took a couple deep breaths and reminded myself that I didn't have to do anything that I didn't want to. I could, in fact, control the situation. Lies. That was a bald faced lie I would continue to tell myself up until Turner came and sat down next to me. Good God, the man smelled divine. It was a subtle soap scent mixed with a light cologne. How bad would it look if I closed my eyes and inhaled?

"Alright I've fed you, given you drinks, and now it's time to talk."

I raised my brow. "About?"

"Annabelle." He said my name in warning.

"Turner." I dished back.

He sighed exasperated. "The baby. Tell me about the baby. It's obvious he means something to you."

Kind of hoped I could dodge this one tonight, but clearly he wasn't going to let me. Now to decide how much to tell him. Would it really hurt if he knew? Turner hasn't shown me any ill will or done anything to make me believe he doesn't want the best for me. He's shown that he just wants to make me happy. Maybe letting him know and actually talking to someone about it would make me feel better and understand a little more myself about these emotions I had.

"Well, you already know about his traumatic birth experience. His mother completely abandoned him not long after she had him, and I just . . . I don't know. I felt bad for him."

"Okay, but you go and see him every time you're on your shift."

I nodded in agreeance. "Yes, sometimes more." I looked down at my pants and picked the lines in the fiber. "It started off as me just wanting to check in on him and making sure the kid was being given a fighting chance. But then, next thing I knew I found myself wandering back in and asking the nurses how he was doing. I felt awful for him that there was no family for him to be held by. The only human contact was what the nurses were capable of giving, and even then, their time has to be split amongst other infants that demanded the same, if not more, of their attention. It just didn't seem fair to me. The way my parents were taken from me so young, I know what it's like to be alone."

He was listening so intently. "Okay, I get that much. So you wanted him to feel love. But do you love him as well?"

I could only answer honestly. "Yes, I suppose I do."

"He's a fragile little person. What you're doing is so beyond selfless, it's admirable. Do you understand how big of a heart you have? We are taught throughout our residency not to get too attached to our patients. It's okay to be empathetic toward them, but getting close was frowned upon. Most of us shut it off. We go in, get the job done, and walk out. I'm sure you've seen that with several doctors that come in to catch the baby, and leave the rest up to you nurses. But this is so much more than that." He put his hand on the hand that was fidgeting. "Annabelle, look at me."

I couldn't fight him asking. I gave him my eyes. "It's commendable."

A lump was forming in my throat and I swallowed. "Is it? Or is it stupid?"

"Why would it be stupid?"

"I don't know. Maybe because he isn't mine. I mean I did get attached. I really have. He has machines helping him breathe, he has tubes pumping food into his stomach so he doesn't have to work so hard to digest anything, and none of it seems fair. I don't know why I chose to spend time with him like I have. It just sort of happened."

He leaned forward and placed a kiss on my forehead. It was sweet. "If it's what feels right, then keep doing it. Besides studies show, that the kind of contact you're giving him helps the healing process."

"I know."

"Then don't question it."

I paused and thought for a second if I should tell him the rest. "I've named him."

"What?"

"I haven't told anybody that, but when I talked to him and I sang to him, I decided he deserved a name instead of just 'Baby March' that is on all his charts. I named him Noah. Seemed fitting."

Aqua blue eyes beamed down at me. "That's a good, strong name."

Totally not the reaction I was expecting from that little confession. Most men would hear about babies, and baby names and get the hell out of dodge. Turner was surprising the hell out of me by not doing what I figured he would when any of this came out. I didn't know whether to hug him for being so understanding, or to question his own sanity for not thinking I was crazy.

"Thank you."

"For what?"

"For having enough gumption to ask. It's not like it's an easy subject for a typical man."

He put his hand on his chest. "Ouch. I'm typical?"

This time I reached out to him. No clue where the bravery came from, but it seemed appropriate. My palm cupped his cheek. "You are anything but typical."

Time stood still. I was lost to him, and how he was making me feel. But then he asked his next question.

"What happened with your parents?"

My arm dropped. Another tough subject. Hadn't we had enough heavy for one night?

"What do you want to know?"

"The night it all happened. Were you there?"

"No. But I was supposed to be."

He frowned. "You were supposed to be?"

"In the car, I mean. My parents had gone to the mountains for their annual 'it's going to be too cold to sleep outside' camping trip. They'd done it since I was a baby. It was the one vacation that all three of us looked forward to every year. I wasn't one of those teens that avoided their parents. I loved being around them. That particular year, I had come down with some crazy flu that my body didn't want to shake. My mom was going to cancel but I told her I'd be fine. The neighbors were near, and I was old enough to drive by then anyway if I needed something. I'll never forget how reluctant she was. My dad said we could hold off for another weekend, but really it was already getting too late in the year and I didn't want to be the reason they missed it for the first time since they started the tradition. I promised I'd have my phone nearby, and if anything happened they would know. They were on their way back from the three day trip. I was finally starting to feel better and was expecting them home later that evening. But there was a knock on my door." I closed my eyes and did everything I could to hold back the tears. I hadn't spoken about this or even allowed myself to think of it for years. The memory was too painful and not the way I wanted to remember them. "I vaguely remember the officer telling me what had happened. They weren't very far from home. Maybe an hour. Someone had been coming off of their long shift and fell asleep at the wheel and they crossed the median. The whole vehicle was totaled. The backseat where I would have been sitting was mangled. Both died on impact. The officer had asked me if there was someone that he could call for me, but there was no one. My grandparents were already gone, and both were only children. They're laid to rest near here but I haven't been back to visit their grave sites since they were buried."

He sat for a moment and let what I'd said sink in. "You were sixteen?"

"Yes."

"Did the courts want to place you in the system?"

"No. Technically I was already ahead of the rest of my class in school, and I was old enough to emancipate myself. My parents left their insurance policies in my name, and the house. I've been on my own since."

"Seriously, Annabelle, that's awful."

I shrugged, not sure what else to say.

"I'm sorry for asking you to tell me. But thank you for trusting me enough to tell me all of this."

I glanced up at him. "Welcome. Hey, where's your bathroom?"

He appeared a little put off by my quick change in subject. Pointing to a door off the living room, he said, "Through there and to the left."

"Thank you."

I stood and went where he directed me. The door he told me to go through was his bedroom. I didn't think about where I was walking, I just wanted to get away and calm down. Being in here wasn't going to help the process. Instead of lingering, I went straight into the bathroom and shut the door, locking it behind me. It was a much larger space than you'd expect from a one bedroom apartment. There was a stand up shower, with a separate Jacuzzi tub in one corner. And in the other, was a door that lead to the toilet. I didn't actually need to go, so I walked to the sink. Turner kept this room very neutral. The walls were white and beige towels hung on the racks. It reminded me of a JCPenny's catalog. Not at all what I'd expect after seeing the rest of the modern space. Guess everyone needed a little bit of dullness in their life.

Turning on the sink, I splashed some water on my face. It was cool and it soothed my frazzled nerves. I'd overshared. I didn't regret telling him, but it was too much for a night like tonight. I had a long day at work, he'd seen me with the baby, and all I really wanted from tonight was a relaxing dinner, wine, and to see if anything else progressed between us. It was already a long time coming. Well, in terms of how quickly I knew he moved. It was a good pace for me though. The conversation had likely put a damper on the evening.

Shutting off the water, I dabbed my face on the bland towel, and walked out the door. What I didn't expect to find was Turner, standing in the doorway, his chest rising and falling a little too fast.

"Are you okay?" I asked.

No answer. Instead he came at me like a freight train. Turner picked me up under my arms leaving me no choice but to wrap my legs around his waist. He didn't stop his forward momentum until he had me pushed up against the wall by the bathroom.

"No, I'm not okay." He breathed in my face. "I need you."

No other conversation was needed. Thoughts of what we discussed only ten minutes ago were out the window. Right now was sheer animal instinct, and I had no intention of stopping him. His mouth came crushing down on mine in a forceful manner that would leave my lips swollen and bruised. Open mouths, tongues battling, and pure desire were swirling in the air, and I knew without a shadow of a doubt that I wasn't going to stop him if he took this as far as it could go tonight. I needed him just like he said he needed me. I wanted him inside of me. I wanted to know how he moved and thrusted. No more imagining the "what if's." I'd take what I wanted from him, and I'd dare him to tell me no.

His tongue pushed against mine with a force that I'd never felt before. He licked and sucked on my lower lip. Nipping when he pulled away and came back for more. I repeated his motions, and I could feel what I was doing to him. The bulge beneath his jeans was enough to make me want to whimper. My hips moved forward and I pressed myself against him. I was wet and I needed relief from the pressure that was stirring in my sex. Setting me down, I stood on my tiptoes still trying to taste his lips.

"I want you on my bed, naked, Annabelle." The way he said my name was so different than any other time.

I ripped my shirt off and unbuttoned my jeans. "More?" I taunted, not knowing where this daring girl had come from.

"All of it. Don't make me ask again."

I backed up until the bed hit the back of my knees. "I don't see you doing the same."

He took two steps in my direction. "You want the shirt gone?"

"Mhmm."

Doing that one-arm over the back of his head move that guys somehow master, he pulled it over his head and tossed it to the side. I stared at every chiseled curve of his abs and ribs. There wasn't even a patch of hair leading below his jeans. The shape of what was threatening to break out from under the zipper was so enticing, my mouth watered.

"What now?"

"Pants, Turner."

He shook his head no. "I believe I asked first."

I twisted around giving him my back. Unzipping, I hooked my thumbs on the top of my jeans and pushed them down my legs. They reached my knees and dropped to the floor. I made a show of stepping out of them and looking over my shoulder. My hair was hanging down past the middle of my back, and I was wearing a pair of black cheeky underwear. Couldn't have been more thankful in that moment that I was a firm believer that pretty underwear, even if nobody saw them, made you feel good during the day.

"You going to make me wait?" I asked, turning around to face him.

The corner of his mouth tipped up into a devilish smile. "Suppose not."

I watched every little move he made as he removed his clothing, leaving him standing in only a pair of dark blue boxer briefs. My legs were weak and I was going to come out of my skin if he didn't touch me soon.

"Come here." He crooked his finger at me, beckoning me to join him.

I shook my head no. "I can't."

And I really couldn't. I was frozen where I stood. Unless he lay me down on this bed behind me, my leaning up against it was the only thing keeping me from falling to my knees and begging him to give me what I wanted. And right now I'd take just about anything from him. It had been entirely too long since I'd been with a man. It should be considered a sin how long it had been.

He got the picture, closed the space between us and pressed his firm body against mine. His skin was warm, while mine felt overheated. His hands came up and grazed the upper part of my arm and slowly descended until he reached my elbow. He grasped me and leaned me back, letting me know he wanted me lying down. I obliged. My back hit a smooth pillowy surface, and my head rested on the comfort of down feathers. He hovered over top of me. Next to the bed was his night stand. He opened the drawer and pulled out a silver wrapper. He made no show of hiding he was grabbing a condom. This was really happening.

"My God, you're beautiful." His eyes roamed over my exposed skin.

The way he was looking down at me, I felt exactly that. Beautiful. Coming down to me, Turner placed his hands on either side of my head and stared at me. It was nearly dark in the room, the only illumination was the moon coming through the floor to ceiling windows and the light from the living room. The music was still playing but I couldn't really hear it. If it was on in the bedroom, it was background noise to the buzzing in my own ears. My clit was throbbing and I needed him to touch me. My panties were drenched. I was regretting not taking them off. He did want me naked after all.

His mouth came down to mine in a reverent and tender manner. He was savoring my lips instead of devouring them. His teeth barely scraped the pouty flesh. I was already worked up. I loved that he was being so attentive, but my need was driving me crazy. My hands took on a life of their own. One smoothed across Turner's cheek and dove into his soft hair, gripping a small handful and pulling him closer, while the other rubbed across his ribs and my nails dragged around to his back. He took the hint. His mouth left mine and traveled their way down my neck leaving a path of sizzling skin and cool wetness from his tongue. He made it to the cup of my bra, and he leaned over enough to use his hand to slide it down underneath my breast. My nipple was peaked and tight. He closed his warm mouth around it and lightly sucked. My body quaked. I felt every sensation of his tongue swirling over the bud, making it even more tender. He was trying to kill me.

"Turner, please, no more. I need you. Stop teasing me."

He didn't release me. Instead, he stayed latched on and showed me his vibrant blue eyes. His pupils dilated from the dark and lust. Never in my life had someone worked me up so much.

"You want more?" He let his hand trail down to the top of my underwear. My hips lifted on their own accord.

"Oh God, yes."

"Are you wet?"

I wasn't much for dirty talk, but if it got him to touch me, I'd become the next best porn star.

"Soaking wet."

"Good girl."

His fingers slipped beneath my underwear and teased the top of my pussy. They skirted my clit which felt so swollen with need, I knew the moment any pressure touched there an orgasm would follow. Turner released my nipple and blew his cool breath across it, causing me to shake.

"Too much, Turner." I felt like my sentences were short and clipped.

He knew I was done. Helping me remove the bit of lace that was in the way, his large fingers made contact with my sex and slipped inside me.

"Jesus, you are soaked," he groaned in my ear.

I couldn't say anything else. Words left me and my body was working solely on instinct and feel. He was driving me to pleasure as if he knew my body better than I knew it myself. His fingers made graceful movements back and forth over my clit. He stroked once, twice, three times, and everything went tense. My first orgasm rolled through me like a subtle crashing wave. It came over the top of me and crested, leaving me panting and breathless.

"Hmmm, that was good, but I think you have more in you," he said, still rubbing the swollen nub.

I took a deep breath and grabbed his wrist to stop his movement. "Hmmm, maybe."

He wanted a fun and flirtatious side of me, I'd give it to him. Deciding to be the aggressor, I put my other hand on his chest and pushed up to allow me to sit up. Flipping over, he took the same position I was just in and now Turner was on his back. I admired the Adonis like body that was laying beneath me. Others I'd been with hadn't really taken care of themselves, not quite like he did. Every little inch of him was sculpted and manicured. He was truly a work of art. Men would kill to have his physique and women drooled over it. Tonight, it was mine, and I wanted to touch him everywhere my eyes could see.

"You tortured me a little bit, do you realize this?" I asked, a devilish gleam on my face.

"I might."

"It wasn't very nice, Doctor Brooks."

"I never claimed to be nice."

"I can see that."

He quirked his brow. "What's that supposed to mean?"

I licked my lips. "I guess you'll just have to wait until I show you exactly how 'nice' you were to me."

Taking my pointer finger, I dragged my nail down the middle of his chest, past his belly button, and to the band of his underwear. Opening my palm, I skimmed it over his erection that was so stiff, I don't know how it didn't hurt him to be trapped like that. Too bad I wasn't willing to free it yet. I did the very thing he did to me. I let my fingers wander around the edges of his throbbing cock and down the inside of his thighs. I saw his dick jump from needing to be touched and being neglected. Several rounds of my teasing and he was getting frustrated. A low growl came from his throat.

"Annabelle, you're testing my resolve."

I nipped at his bare nipple. "Yeah? What are you going to do about it?"

In less than a second I was flat on my back again, and Turner taken his place on top of me. He took his briefs off and reached for the condom on the night stand.

I smirked. "Want me to do it?"

"No." I could hear the impatience in this voice.

I wasn't offended in the least. I knew why he sounded the way that he did, and I didn't think I had the patience to do the work myself. As he rolled the rubber down his shaft, I looked him over when he got fully naked. His dick was certainly bigger than expected, but the girth was something I briefly wondered if it would hurt. All thoughts disappeared when Turner held his cock in his hand, and was at my entrance. I knew this wasn't going to take very long for me. My skin was on fire, and he looked like he was ready to take on Mount Everest with that determination.

"Let me know if I hurt you."

I nodded.

Pushing the head in, I closed my eyes and let myself feel every inch and he slowly sank inside me. It was a tantalizing pleasure that I didn't want to end, but needed so much more of. When he was seated fully inside, Turner grabbed my hips and lifted them so my butt was no longer on the bed. It allowed for deeper penetration, and his cock rubbed against something inside of me I'd never felt before. A moan tore from my throat.

"You good?"

I opened my eyes and saw the feral look in his. "Yes."

"Good, cause I'm about to open it up."

What was he talking about? And then I knew. His slow and steady became a more rhythmic pace that had my body soaring. The tip of his cock was sliding over my G-spot and something huge was forming in my lower stomach. The faster he went the more my breasts bounced, and he watched everything. He was getting off on seeing them move, and my face as it morphed into insatiable pleasure. I needed to come, and I felt like I was standing at the top of a hill with a boulder needing to push it over the edge, but I wasn't quite there yet.

My nails dug into Turners thighs, and sweat glistened across his chest. I knew what I wanted. "Harder." I demanded.

A groan bubbled out of him. He was holding back his own pleasure, waiting for me to finish with my own. "Yes, ma'am."

Turner slammed into me, pushing my head back further on the bed. That's exactly what I'd been waiting for.

"Oh my God, yes."

"Now, Annabelle."

An orgasm so intense washed through me and my body felt electrified. I said words that were incoherent to even me, and Turner came forward on his hands, unable to stay on his knees like he had been. I felt him push in as far as he could go and as my orgasm pulsed, his hit him. He said my name into my hair, and his thighs tensed. Turner exhaled loudly, and breathed deep. Wrapping my arms around his wide back. I smoothed the sweat, and comforted his overworked muscles.

"You okay?" He mumbled, clearly too weak to move just yet. It made me smile.

"I'm more than okay."

He grunted, and I laughed.

"Woman, no," he scolded.

"What?"

"You squeeze when you laugh like that. I can't handle it."

Oh. I wanted to giggle over the sheer silliness that he felt that sensitive, but honestly if he started to move, I'd probably roll into another small orgasm. We stayed quiet for a while, listening to each other breathe, and taking in what we'd just done. My eyes were heavy. Eventually, he rolled off of me, and he stood walking to the bathroom. The light illuminated the room, and I watched as he took the used condom off and tossed it in the trash. When he came back to the bed, he lay down beside me and pulled me into him. I was never one for cuddling, but this was nice. I felt safe here. It was a good spot.

"Thank you for sharing things with me today. I know it wasn't easy, but I needed you to let me in, Annabelle."

He was right. I did. There was no judgement when I told him about the baby and my parents, just an open mind and understanding.

"You're welcome."

"Close your eyes, sweet girl. I know you're exhausted."

I sank further into him, his arm resting on my hip and my head on his chest. "Hmmmm, I am."

As I let sleep take me, I told myself, this night was going to go down as one of the best nights of my life. Happiness consumed me, and I was feeling untouchable. No fear. This was how one should live.

CHAPTER TEN

Annabelle

I WOKE UP THE NEXT MORNING in Turner Brook's bed. If that wasn't an aphrodisiac all on its own I didn't know what was. A man that so many women desired, I brought to his knees. Last night was incredible. Plus, I don't think I'd slept so well in years. Not because this bed was particularly comfortable, but because Turner used my body and made me feel things I'd never felt before.

He wasn't in bed with me when I blinked my eyes open and stretched my arms above my head. I was deliciously sore. Wonder where he was. My nose picked up on the scent of coffee just as the thought crossed my mind. Kitchen, he was in the kitchen. Sitting up, I looked around the room. In the light of day, things appeared a little different. Okay, maybe not really since I hadn't actually spent much time checking out the room before Turner was on me demanding nakedness. I was currently lying in a king size bed that had a dark gray duvet covering my bare body. This space was a little more industrial than the living space. A wooden dresser was against the wall opposite the bed, and it had a particular hardware on the front for handles. There wasn't really a finish to it, it was simple and masculine. The floors were a dark gloss, but not exactly black tile. The floor to ceiling windows opened the space and looked out over part of Athens, and part of a popular park that sat in the middle of the city. The view was stunning. I'm sure he paid high dollar for a place like this. I wondered if he rented or owned.

I needed to put some clothes on and get the first cup of coffee flowing through my veins. Not thinking much of it, I padded over to Turner's dresser and opened the top drawer hoping to find what I was looking for. Bingo. A basic white t-shirt sat on top, and I pulled it out. I hoped he didn't mind, but I didn't feel like putting on my clothes from the night before just yet. The shirt was definitely a little baggy on me, and fell to my mid-thigh. Looking in the mirror before I walked out, I gasped. Bright eyes stared back at me, and pink cheeks. I looked . . . vibrant. That's the only thing that came to mind. My hair could use a brush, but my fingers would have to be good enough for now. Wow, I barely recognized myself. I grinned. This was a good look.

When I opened the bedroom door, Turner was standing in the kitchen leaning over the counter staring at a newspaper. His eyes caught mine as I stepped into the space.

"Morning." I tucked my hair behind my ear, and looked down.

"Good morning." He strode to me and tilted my chin up toward him. "How'd you sleep?"

I briefly wondered if I had morning breath. "Well, actually."

"Mmm, good." He bent forward and kissed my lips tenderly. "Coffee?"

I smiled. "Yes, please."

He released me from his hold and walked back to the kitchen. Getting a mug from the cupboard, he poured me a cup and asked if I needed cream or sugar. I nodded. He set everything out and let me fix it the way I liked. He watched what I was doing, and I wondered if he was taking notes in case I stayed again.

Turner was leaning against the counter looking edible. He was wearing a fitted shirt, and a pair of gym shorts. I guess he got up and went for a jog.

"You want something to eat? I can make us eggs and bacon. Pretty sure I have everything for pancakes as well."

My bare feet made no sound as I went around the island to the bar stool. "No, you don't need to go to any trouble. Coffee is usually pretty sufficient for me."

"You sure? 'Cause I also have . . ." He made a show of grabbing a box of cereal out from a small pantry. "My favorite, of course."

I giggled. "Of course. Fruity Pebbles, why didn't I think of that?" I shook my head. "As good as those look and I haven't had them in forever, I think I'm okay."

He set it on the counter. "Okay, well if you change your mind, I'll leave the box out."

I took a sip of the extra hot coffee. "Thank you."

Folding up his paper, he kept looking up at me with a funny expression.

"What?"

The side of his mouth tipped up. "You look good in my shirt, Annabelle. I should see you like this more often."

Tilting my head to the side I felt heat creep into my cheeks. "Is that so?"

"Yes, ma'am. Even in the morning, just woken up, you look perfect."

I twisted the mug in my hands. "I don't know about all of that, but you are being awfully sweet this morning."

"Pretty sure we established that that's one of my many admirable qualities."

My eyes shot up to his. "One of many," I admitted with a smirk.

He let me sit and drink my coffee, while he picked up the kitchen from whatever he left out last night. There wasn't really a mess, just more him straightening and us once again enjoying the other's quiet presence. I liked watching him move about his space. For such a large man, he was very graceful and meticulous. Being a doctor was a very good career choice for him. His hands were flawless. I don't think he even realized how methodical he was.

"So what would you like to do today?" he asked, breaking the silence.

I didn't realize he wanted to spend another day together. I thought about it. "I don't know, actually. It's nice outside, but I don't really wander too much."

"Well, we've already established that you don't know how to drive a standard vehicle."

The statement seemed completely out of the blue, but there was a gleam in his eyes that told me he already had an idea before he mentioned anything.

"Noooo, I don't." I drew out.

"Good. We have plans then. We can stop by your house for a change of clothes. You're going to want to wear something with long sleeves and jeans."

"Turner, it's not that cold outside."

He grinned. "Oh, it will be with the top off on the Jeep. You're going to learn how to drive my baby today. I need to go get cleaned up. Make yourself at home, grab some more coffee if you'd like—eat something too, please. I won't be long."

My mouth was hanging open. Was he kidding? What made him think that I could drive the Jeep? I knew it was a standard but honestly, I had no interest in learning. He drove it just fine. Riding with the top off was the only appealing part of this little excursion. And where did he plan on taking me to do this? I was bound to hit something or somebody. I swear to God, I wouldn't be held responsible for any damage to his vehicle or a human. This was nuts.

Turner came back out of the bedroom freshly wash, hair spiked every which way from being wet and looking sexy as ever. He had on a gray, long sleeved shirt, and a pair of worn jeans. He looked like he was ready to go off-roading or to get dirty. It was mouth-watering.

"You ready to go?"

"Uhhhh, sure?" I said confused.

"Grab your clothes and let's head out." He picked up his keys and put his wallet in his back pocket.

Looks like I didn't have much choice in the matter. But have I had a choice with him since we started this whole thing? Sighing, I knew better than to argue. I went to the bedroom and put my clothes on from the night before. When we got down to the jeep, Turner jumped into the driver's seat and we took off down the road, headed to my house to I could get cleaned up too.

"There are some dirt roads about fifteen miles down the way. We'll switch spots there," he shouted over the wind in my ears.

The top was down, and at the speed we were cruising, it was definitely cool. I didn't feel like responding or yelling loud enough for him to hear me so I kept my mouth shut and waited 'til we got to where we were going. Turner had a nice sound system in here and it played over the sound noise of the wind whipping around. My hair blew across my face and I reached up and tied it into a ponytail to keep it all back. I was going to look a mess by the end of the day. It didn't take long until we were pulling off to the side of the road and there were trails of dirt and hills. This looked more like a dirt bike road than something you'd drive a Jeep on.

"Here?" I asked.

"Yep, here." He grinned. Turner pulled forward and pulled the parking break up. "You ready?" He unbuckled his seatbelt and looked at me expectantly.

"So you really want me to do this?"

"Yes, ma'am."

"Any way I could talk you out of it? I'm not really in the mood to give you, or me, whiplash today." I came across grumpy.

"Turn that frown upside down. It's easier than you think. Hop out and switch spots with me."

I did as he asked, and apprehensively buckled back up.

"Okay, I'm sure you understand the concept of the gears. The thing you need to pay attention to and feel is when the RPM's hit between these two numbers. You'll hear the engine rev and that's when you shift. Got that so far?"

I nodded.

"Push your left foot down on the clutch 'til it's on the floor." He watched me do it. "Now, I want you to slowly give it some gas. It's going to be like an equal give and take." Turner was showing me hand motions trying to explain. "It's okay if the gas revs the engine while you're in first gear. As you gradually remove your foot from the clutch, the Jeep will move forward. You ready to try?"

My palms were sweaty. "No."

He chuckled, placing his hand on my forearm giving it a squeeze. "Relax, this is fun and you'll be surprised how easy it really is."

"That's what you say now," I mumbled under my breath.

"What's that?"

"Nothing," I said rolling my eyes.

Having my first go, I visualized the motions he made with his hands. "It's an equal give and take." Right. My foot was pressed into the clutch, and I slowly gave it some gas. As the engine roared, I gently began releasing my foot from the clutch. The Jeep crept forward a couple of inches, and I got excited.

"We're moving!" I smiled.

Clearly getting too excited, I did things a little faster than I was ready for. I picked my left foot up before there was enough gas being given and the Jeep jerked forward, hard. Turner uttered something along the lines of "gas, gas, gas." Too late of course. We stalled.

He rubbed his hands together. "Again."

I looked over at him. "Are you crazy? I'm going to break your damn Jeep. This was the dumbest idea you've had so far, which is saying something 'cause we've done some insane shit, Turner."

The belly rolling laugh that came out of him almost made me want to crack a smile, but I held my ground. "Do you know how many times I stalled before I actually was able to shift out of first gear? I thought my dad's transmission was going to fall out. No quitting. Go again."

I sighed. Much like the first time, I stalled again. And then again, and again. I slapped my hands on the steering wheel and cursed under my breath. This was one of the most frustrating things I think I'd ever tried to do in my life. If he told me I "could do it" one more time I swear, Turner Brooks was going to go home with a black eye.

"Alright, listen, I know it's aggravating. Give it one more try. If it doesn't work, we can switch spots and I'll take you for a spin around the trails."

"Fine." I know my tone was that of a petulant child, but I didn't care. Had I been standing I might have even stomped my foot on the ground.

Taking a deep breath, I tried to recenter myself. Doing everything he instructed of me when we first tried all of this, I took my time and was determined to at least make it into second gear. As if I willed it to happen, the vehicle moved. When it started to shake, I gave it some gas and I was finally able to make the shift. I squealed.

"Oh my God, I did it." I lifted both my feet off the pedals and the Jeep shot forward and died. I busted out laughing. "Crap."

He was grinning ear to ear, and looking at me like I was the most entertaining person on the planet. "You're cute, you know that?"

"I'm cute?" I was still giggling. "You won't think I'm so cute when I make *your* transmission fall out."

He shook his head. "Nah."

It got quiet and he was staring at me.

"What?"

"Nothing, I just think you're a pretty special girl."

I tilted my head to the side. "What do you mean?"

"You're not like others that I've dated before, Annabelle. You're just . . . different is all. Take it as a compliment."

Heat creeped up my cheeks. "Thank you then."

I didn't know how else to respond. It was sweet how he said the words.

"Okay, want me to take you for a real spin now?"

I smiled, not even thinking twice about the danger or how I could possibly be scared. In this moment I was free and Turner was the one who held the key to that freedom. "Let's go."

It was an absolute blast. Never in my life had I felt so unguarded and careless. It was life and it was enjoyable. I had a boyfriend who was nothing short of amazing, a gratifying job, Noah was getting stronger by the minute, and friends that were truly there for me whenever I needed them. I was happy.

CHAPTER ELEVEN
Turner

MY GOD, SHE WAS BEAUTIFUL. Hovering over the top of me, the wind lightly blowing her strawberry blonde hair past her face. She had a sheen of sweat across her brow from exertion and a smile that I had a feeling couldn't be wiped from her face if someone tried. This was the happiest I'd seen her. Walls were down, heart was open, and I imagine this is the Annabelle that probably existed before her parents died. The world was blessed to have her. In this moment, I knew without a shadow of a doubt, I would do everything in my power to make sure she stayed this way for the rest of her days. She deserved this kind of freedom to be who she really is. If I saw her closing off the world, I'd make sure she let go and saw there was nothing to fear. I would be that for her.

"What are you smiling about?" I goaded her.

She bent down, my dick still buried inside her. She kissed the tip of my nose and said, "Nothing and everything."

"Good. That's the way it should be."

Annabelle sat up and looked around her. She was searching for her clothes, which were a couple feet away. On shaky legs, I watched as she slid me out of her, and stood. Her body was incredible. Curves in all the right places and nothing but perfection to my eyes. I reached down and took the condom off, tying the end. Unlike her shyness from the last time, there was no reservation as she stood in front of me in all her gorgeousness. She dressed herself not caring that I was staring at her. I couldn't take it anymore. After I taught her how to drive my Jeep, I needed her right then and there, so I took what I wanted.

"What is it, Doctor Brooks?"

"Just enjoying the view."

She bit her lip. I swear if she didn't stop, she was going to have to get naked all over again.

"Hmmm, yes. it is beautiful out here." Her aqua eyes roamed the area.

"I see nothing but you."

She picked up my shirt and tossed it in my face, giggling. "Get dressed charmer."

I got up and put my clothes back on. She folded the blanket we'd been on while I walked over to the Jeep. Annabelle's phone started ringing the second I got near. I glanced at the screen and saw it was the hospital, but ignored it. It was her day off. They were probably calling to ask her to do overtime or cover someone's shift. Not today. Today, she was mine. I went around to the driver's side and checked my own phone. Hers went off again. What on earth? I picked it up and called over to Annabelle.

"Hey, the hospital is trying to call. Want me to answer?"

She came toward me at a leisurely pace. She looked completely satisfied.

"Sure. If they want me to come in, tell them no." She laughed at herself.

I swiped my finger to pick up the call.

"Hello, Doctor Brooks. "

"Doctor Brooks? Oh sorry, I was trying to get in touch with Annabelle, is she around?"

"She is, but she isn't able to come to the phone at the moment."

"Oh, okay. Well, this is Lauren, one of the NICU nurses. I care of the little boy she frequently visits."

There was a tone in her voice that had me more alert. "I know who you are, Lauren. What's going on?"

She sighed into the phone, reluctant to tell me. "The baby . . . he, uh, he went into cardiac arrest earlier this morning and, unfortunately, the doctors weren't able to get him back into a regular arrhythmia. He passed away around noon. We knew she'd want to know."

My heart sank. Everything around me came crashing down.

"Oh shit. Okay, well, thank you for calling." It may have been rude, but I hung up.

I watched as Annabelle came toward me, the smile still in place from only moments ago and I was about to deliver news to her that would send her spiraling. How the hell was I going to tell her this? She was good. She was happy. Noah dying was something that would send every guarded wall and barrier right back up in place with steel walls. How would I deal with her then? It didn't matter. My needs were selfish. I had to tell her.

"What did they want? A nurse need the day off and want me to come in?" She said it like it was her own personal joke.

"Annabelle." I said her name. It was enough to cause her to stop moving. Concern etched her face.

"What? What is it?"

I wasn't going to hold it back from her any longer than necessary. "That was Lauren from the NICU. She called to let you know something."

Her voice shook. "What the hell is it, Turner?"

"It's Noah. He developed an arrhythmia. He didn't make it, baby."

It didn't take a genius to see that she was about to collapse. I rounded the Jeep and caught her just before she hit the ground. I went down with her in my arms. I adjusted her so I was cradling her, brushing back her hair that had fallen forward.

"I don't understand."

I looked into eyes that were so confused and wanting to cry but couldn't produce tears yet.

"I know. Unfortunately, sometimes these things happen. It could have been anything."

Her head tossed back and forth and denial seeped in. "No, these things don't just happen. He was fine. I was just with him yesterday morning. The doctor told me he was doing better. His stats were good, they were going to decrease some of his medication. This doesn't make any sense. Are they sure they called the right person?"

I lowered my head to hers. "I'm sorry, Annabelle. What can I do?"

She didn't answer me. She simply looked off into the distance and kept her mouth shut. She wasn't here with me. She was somewhere else. Remembering something, feeling something, and I wasn't included. I stood with her in my arms and I set her in the passenger seat.

"Do you want me to take you home, or would you like to come back to my place?"

Again, silence.

I didn't know what to do. A new side of Annabelle was emerging and this was one that I had no clue how to deal with. I wasn't familiar with death. Even worse, I didn't know how to handle death of a baby. Tentatively I buckled her in and came back to the driver's side. I had no clue where I was going so I did the one thing that I felt was right. I drove her back to her house. It was a quiet drive. Nothing could be said. We were only just outside of the city and it was maybe twenty minutes, but when your head is full of unanswered questions and wondering why these things happened to good people, it made for an extraordinarily long ride. When I pulled into her driveway, I grabbed her keys from her purse and went to unlock the door. She wasn't following behind me, so I went back to the Jeep and carried her inside. Her cat, Chaz, came running but didn't meow like he normally did. Even he could tell his human wasn't okay.

Setting her on her bed, I slipped her shoes off and asked her if she needed anything. There was no response. She lay down and faced the wall. I don't think I'd ever felt so helpless in my life. Did I lay down beside her and cuddle her and let her feel me there with her? Did I leave her alone and check on her later? Did I go into the kitchen and make something for her and see if she would eat? What the in the hell was the right thing here? I chose the first option. Scooting in behind her, I wrapped my arm around her middle and pulled her back to my chest. I felt her breathe in deep and exhale. She still hadn't shed a single tear, which I found more disturbing than her silence. I knew she was feeling broken from the news, but the way she loved Noah, there was bound to be a river of tears waiting to come crashing out of her, it was just a matter of time. She needed to cry. I brushed my thumb back and forth in a soothing fashion across her stomach, and I waited for something to hit me. I hoped sleep would claim her for at least a little bit. In the meantime, I would also wait for some guidance to what I needed to be doing.

Sleep did take her under after she shifted around restlessly for almost a half hour. I quieted her the best I could, and her cat jumped on the bed in front of her and purred in her face. I think he gave her more comfort than I was capable of giving her. When I felt her heavy breathing, I carefully moved out of the bed without disturbing her and did the next best thing I could think of. Stepping outside, I called my mom.

"Hey, baby, whatchu up too?" My mom's southern drawl was always sugary sweet when she heard from her boys.

"Mom, something happened."

I could hear her moving and shutting a door. "Sorry, I had some company over. What's going on, Turner?"

"You remember that baby Annabelle told you about? The one she cared for?"

"Of course."

"She got a call today that he died."

Mom gasped. "Sweet Jesus, what happened? How is Annabelle doing?"

"Honestly, we don't know many details, but he's gone." I swallowed hard. I, myself, was getting choked up. "She's not doing well, Mom. She won't speak and she hasn't cried."

It took her a moment to respond. "Okay, well we all grieve differently."

"No, Mom, you don't get it. She's lost. I can see it in her eyes, she's not there right now. As soon as I told her, everything shut off and she receded. I don't know what to do."

"Alright, baby, it's okay. Tell me where are you at and I'll come to y'all. She may need another female to confide in. It's not you, but she's a very guarded girl. I could tell from the start. I can see where this would make her shut down."

Maybe she was right. Maybe Annabelle needed a woman to talk to. I might not be the source of comfort she was seeking.

I gave her the address and told her to come whenever she'd like, but that Annabelle was sleeping right now and probably needed it. She agreed and said she would be over in a couple hours. I figured that was plenty of time to get myself together and figure out what my girl needed.

Time was flying by, yet slowed every time I looked at the clock. Annabelle was still in bed. She'd woken once and I went in to ask her if she was hungry, and got her a glass of water with some aspirin. She declined all of it. Only two words had been uttered by her since we left the field, and I was now anxious for my mom to get here to see what she could do.

About that time, the doorbell rang. Annabelle looked over at me and I gave her a sympathetic look.

"I called my mom. I'm sorry if that makes you upset, but I think you need someone other than just me right now."

She simply nodded.

Going to the door, I let my mom in and took her purse. "Where is she?"

"Down the hall, the last door on the left."

Taking no time to ask me anything else, she headed off in the direction I told her. I followed behind her. Upon entering the room, Annabelle was still lying down but facing the door. Her expression appeared to be resolved. She knew she was going to be asked questions and it was like she had steeled herself for the onslaught. Except, that's not what happened. My mom, in her typical fashion knew exactly what was needed. She took one look at Annabelle, and instead of the fifty questions I think both of us expected, she went to her and lifted her head and lay Annabelle's head back down in her lap. I watched on as my mother gently stroked Annabelle's hair and started to hum a soft lullaby I knew she sang to my brothers and me when we were younger and not feeling well.

She cracked.

Tears pooled in her eyes, and for the first time in hours, she released her emotions. My mom cooed to her and told her it would be okay. She simply let her have her feelings without forcing anything from her. It was then that I knew I made the right choice asking her to come over. Annabelle needed a mom. She needed the touch of a mother to make her feel like her world would be okay even though she was hurting.

"I named him. Turner was the only one I told." Her voice was hoarse from sleep, and not speaking.

"You did? Well, I'm sure it was a special one," my mom replied.

"Noah. It was my dad's middle name."

I didn't know that. She never shared that bit of information with me.

"Noah is a good and strong name. Sounds like he was a fighter."

A fresh wave of tears and sobs wracked her body. "He was, except now he's gone."

"I don't know what your religion is, honey, but I am a firm believer that God has a plan for all of us. When it's our time to be called back to his side, it's because we are needed elsewhere, and to teach those of us who still remain how to live differently. Noah had his purpose. What the purpose was . . . well, that's up to you to search for that answer."

I could tell she was pondering this thought. I didn't think Annabelle was a very religious person, but in some way shape or form, we all had our beliefs. If my mom's words were giving her comfort, then by God, I hope she kept talking. I didn't want to continue to intrude on their moment of quietness and solitude, so I stepped back and shut the door. Walking into the living room, I sat down on the couch and buried my head in my hands, my fingers diving into my hair. My mom being here was giving me some peace as well. I didn't want to deal with this alone and being at a loss how to comfort the one person you never want to see hurt is more stressful than I ever thought possible. Sitting back, I rested my head on the back of the couch and closed my eyes. What a day it has been.

Not having a clue how long it'd been, I awoken by my mom's hand on my leg and her whispered voice telling me she was leaving. I didn't even realize I'd dozed off.

"Where is she?"

Her eyes were red, and I knew she had shed tears alongside my girl. "She's asleep again."

I nodded. "Thanks for coming."

"You're welcome, son."

"I didn't know what else to do, Mom. It's like as soon as I told her he was gone, so was she."

She reached forward and patted my cheek, her hand lingering. "I don't know what it's like losing a child. Hearing Annabelle talk about that baby during dinner, there was so much adoration in her voice, I knew he was special to her." Mom dropped her hand. "She was loving him like he was hers, Turner. I don't know how or why she attached herself to him, but she obviously saw a reason to. The poor girl has seen entirely too much loss in her short life, and this was just another notch for her to believe the world is a cruel place that only hurts her if she lets it."

"Well, I don't need her shutting me out. That's what I'm concerned about right now. It has taken some time to get her to open up to me, and even then she is guarded."

"She has reason to be."

"I know."

Mom gave me a soft smile. "One thing at a time, Turner. You can't fix everyone. Show her you're here, and she will tell you what she needs."

She stood and went for the door.

"You okay to drive, or should I call Dad to come pick you up?"

"I'm good. I'll be calling tomorrow morning to check on her. I have some things I'd like to do, and I'll need your opinion on it."

My mom, always busy doing something. "Sounds good."

She shut the door behind her and the house went silent. What a shitty ending to a day that had so much potential.

Deciding I needed to see Annabelle and feel her, I went back to her room. She was on her back with her hands resting across her stomach. At least she looked peaceful. Stripping off my shirt, I went to her and scooted in beside her. I didn't want to crowd her, but I also wanted to make sure she knew I was here. I placed my hand on top of hers, and of their own accord, her fingers threaded through mine. She breathed in a broken inhale. The kind that comes from a child that had been crying too much. I was giving her space and, yet, still being close enough that if she needed me I was at arms length. It was enough, for now.

CHAPTER TWELVE

Annabelle

IT'D BEEN TWO DAYS since Noah passed. My shifts at the hospital had been picked up and I'd sequestered myself to my house. I didn't want to go anywhere and I didn't want to do anything. I couldn't get over something like this. A baby, who was completely innocent and brought into this world under some of the worst circumstances, fought so hard. He fought and started to get better and then he was snatched away like he didn't matter to anybody. Except he did. He mattered to *me*. I cared enough about him that I'd devoted my time to him, and I loved him and showed him love. His worthless mother abandoned him. No child deserved such cruelty. I didn't have any intention of adopting him or anything, but I would have ensured that someone worthy would have ended up with him. I was nowhere near ready to have a child of my own. In fact, the very idea of having a baby scared me so much I had come to the conclusion that I likely wouldn't have my own kids. I'd seen so many babies being brought into this world. The way the parents react to their new little bundles kept the saying in perspective.

Having a child is like having your heart walking around outside your body.

I had too many nervous tendencies since my parents passed away, to even consider having children. Turner has hardly left my side since I got the news. I didn't know how to speak to him about my grief. I tried yesterday, but nothing came out of my mouth. So I continued on with head nods and shakes as my form of communication and doing the things that others expect from you to show that you're okay. I learned far too early that when someone passes away, the people around you want and need you to be okay, so that they may move on with their own lives. Was it selfish of them? I had no clue. But I could also tell Turner may be on to me. He didn't just watch me, he studied me. It should have made me uncomfortable him being here, but it didn't. His presence was nice, and he never once forced me to talk about anything. He didn't ask me to cry, or tell him how I was feeling. He's simply let me be. But I knew he sensed me. There was something there under the surface of those blue eyes that were watching me. For now, he let me know he was near and it was enough.

Today was just another day that I woke up with the same empty feeling I'd felt the last three days. No Noah, and the fear that life could take a tragic turn for me or anybody else I knew. I rolled over in my bed and smelled that a fresh pot of coffee had been made. Frowning, I sat up and rubbed my eyes. Living like this wasn't ideal for anyone. It was time to make face with Turner, just so I could come back into my room and sleep some more. As I left my comfortable bed, I glanced in the mirror on my way out.

Ewwww, holy crap!

I had a nest forming on the top of my head that would be perfect for a couple baby birds, and I had dark circles under my eyes. I tried to run my fingers through my thick hair, but had no luck. They got stuck in the tangles and I gave up. Lifting my shoulders and exhaling, it didn't matter. Turner wouldn't stick around too much longer. He was going to get tired of my attitude and leave.

"Morning, beautiful." Turner greeted me. He was leaning up against the kitchen counter, shirtless, a pair of sweat pants hanging low on his hips. Could that V get any deeper? Even in my state of mind, I was fully capable of appreciating the man that stood before me. He twisted behind himself to hand me a mug. The simple motion caused my lips to part. When he handed it to me, his blue eyes held mine. There was a warm fire just under the surface that I could see burning. Oh my.

"Morning," I rasped.

He took a sip of his coffee and asked, "How'd you sleep?"

I shook off the errant thoughts and answered, "Like I have been."

"Restless?"

I frowned. "No. Dreamlessly."

He set his mug down. "Sounds boring."

What in the hell? "Sorry to bore you." I went to the coffee pot and poured my first cup.

"Annabelle, you're not boring me. You're misunderstanding what I'm saying. Get your coffee and come out on the deck."

He walked out the sliding glass door, and left me standing there to figure out what he was doing.

I dumped some cream and sugar into my "Follow your dreams" mug. The irony wasn't lost on me, and walked in the same direction he did. Turner was sitting in my dad's chair. I stopped and analyzed how I felt seeing him sitting there. That was a special seat, and only someone who meant something to me should ever be allowed to sit there. After my parents died, all of the distant family and friends that came in and out of this house, I guarded that chair with my life. Nobody was to sit there except my dad or me. And since he was gone, it was only a place for me. A thousand emotions swirled through me, but not a single one was anger or the urge to tell him he needed to move. Turner was welcome there, and I was more than okay with it.

"You going to stand there watching me, or do you plan on coming over here to talk to me?"

I raised my brow despite him not being able to see it. "Are you always so bossy and demanding?"

"No. I could be worse," he said matter of fact.

Great. Lord only knows what that was really like. I came to stand in front of him and made a show of leaning against the railing and feigning indifference to his sassy mouth.

"What's up?"

He wanted to chuckle but he didn't. Instead his expression turned stoic. "We are going to do something a little different. I know you probably want to have your coffee and go lay back down and drown out the day, but not today."

My heart picked up its pace. "What are you talking about, Turner?"

"When you're done with your little breakfast there. . ." He nodded toward my cup. "I'm going to need you to go take a nice long shower, relax your muscles, and get ready for the day. I'll put some clothes out for you. We have somewhere we need to be this morning."

I was already feeling defensive. He wasn't going to force me out of my home just because he didn't want to stay here. "No. You can go do whatever it is that you need to do, but I'm not in the mood to do anything."

"I'm not asking, Annabelle."

"Neither am I." I squared my shoulders.

He sighed, looking slightly defeated. "Please. I'm not going to make you do anything that you don't want to do, but this is something that I think you need."

"And what's that?"

He shook his head. "I'm not saying. You'll fight me tooth and nail, and, frankly, I don't think you are ready for that battle."

"I'm not in the mood for one of your crazy ass dates, Turner."

He almost looked offended. "I'm not taking you on a date."

Okay, now I was confused. If he wasn't taking me on a crazy date, where else would he need to drag me kicking and screaming?

"I need to have an idea of what is going on, okay? I'll admit I'm feeling anxious about stepping foot outside of my comfort zone. You must at least understand that much."

His eyes softened. "I do. We are meeting up with my mom. She asked me to bring you somewhere, and I promised I would. So would you please? If not for me, at least try for her?"

The mother card was now in play. What on earth could Donna have in store for me today? She'd stopped by a few times, maybe even more while I was sleeping, to check on me. She was the only one I'd confided in with my true feelings about Noah. She was a mom of four boys. There was something very maternal going on deep in my bones when it came to the baby. It was unexpected, but she opened her mind to why I felt the way that I did. She shared stories with me how she thought when Camden was born something horrible was happening to him. Turns out, he had an irregular heartbeat and a small murmur. When it's your baby and they aren't the epitome of health, your world stops. You question why these things are happening to you and your baby. Noah may not have been mine, but I did love him. I felt drawn to him the moment he was born and his own mother didn't want to give him a name. I promised myself before I walked out of that delivery room that I would show him what a gentle touch was. Donna praised me for loving unconditionally. She said it was very much the sign of a mother. I wouldn't call myself that at all, but if there was a step below that . . . that was me.

Since it was for Donna, I didn't fight him. I held my cup in both of my hands and nodded. Standing, Turner took a step toward me and placed his lips on my forehead. I closed my eyes and savored the feeling. He was so warm, while I felt so cold. When he pulled away, he went back into the house giving me time to myself, as if I didn't already have an abundance of it. I tossed the rest of my coffee over the railing, not feeling like stomaching the rest. Shower time.

It took me no time at all to get washed up. Although my hair was clearly in the mood to fight today. I won. When I came out of the steaming shower with a towel wrapped around me, Turner had made good on his word—a pair of black dress pants and a deep burgundy, three-quarter length top laid on the bed. This was a bit more fancy than I had expected. Where were we going? I sighed. Probably lunch at the country club or something. Anything for Donna to get me out of the house. I'd appease her. I was in no mood to mess with putting on make-up though. I threw my hair up while it was still wet, slapped on some clear gloss, and went out to the living room. Turner had already gotten dressed. He was wearing a pair of black slacks and a white button down dress shirt. Was this really how they dressed at the country club? I'd never been to one, so maybe. I've read some things about them being stuffy.

"You look nice." Turner complimented me when I came into view.

"Thank you. So do you."

He stood and grabbed his keys. "Alright, let's head out."

I wanted to ask where we were headed, but I knew he wouldn't answer. If I was to know where I was going, I'd know by now. He texted someone while we were still in the driveway, but then set his phone down and we took off down the road. I assumed it was his mom. The ride was silent. I honestly had nothing to say. I closed my eyes and relaxed my slightly frazzled body. Being out of the safety of my home was a little more daunting than I had envisioned it being. Every car that passed, made me wonder if they'd cross the double lines and run head on into us. Every curve that Turner took, I questioned if he was going too fast and we'd flip. Closing my eyes to the outside world was the only way I was going to survive this trip.

I had no concept of time, which direction we were going, or what my surroundings looked like. But when I felt the car ease to a stop and I opened my eyes and saw where I was, every single emotion a human being could have raced through me. I felt Turner's eyes on me, but I swear if I said anything right no, it wouldn't be pretty. How could he? How could Donna? I scanned the grounds. I knew where I was, but how did they know? Did they research? I supposed it wouldn't take much. It's not like these things weren't printed in the newspapers when it happened.

"Annabelle?" he quietly asked.

I swallowed. My throat was dry and I wanted to cough. No scratch that, I wanted to *puke*. I never came here. He knew this.

"Annabelle." He repeated.

Rows and rows of headstones lined the immaculate green grass. It was hilly just like I remembered it, and we were a ways out of the city. The sky was bright blue, but the air was crisp and cool, a warning that fall was not far in the distance. It would be almost beautiful if it was any other place besides a cemetery. I hadn't been here in years. In fact, not since the day my parents were put in the ground.

"No, Turner." My voice shook.

He reached for my hand and I pulled away. "Listen, I know this is probably a shock to you, but I think there's something you need to see."

"There's nothing for me to see, get me the hell out of here."

"No."

"Are you fucking kidding me? I don't want to be here."

He raised his brow. I'd never said that word in front of him before, and me saying it made him realize I was serious. "I'm standing behind bringing you here, so would be you please follow me?"

"I'm out. You won't take me back home, I'm walking." I got out of the car and slammed the door. I only got a few feet away when I heard his door close and he was in front of me, blocking my only exit out of the black iron gates.

"So help me, Annabelle, I will throw you over my shoulder and carry you over there, but I'm asking you to not make me do that."

I furrowed my brow. "Carry me where? I told you the other night I never wanted to step foot here again. There's no purpose."

"There is now. Get your ass moving." He was getting pissed.

The nerve of him. "Don't you dare get pissed off at me. You had no business bringing me here. Seriously, I fucking confide in you, tell you things I've never told a soul, I *trusted* you. And you go off and do the one thing that is so damn cruel and insensitive." I went to march around him, but stopped when I heard Donna's voice.

"It wasn't him, honey, it was me. He's only doing what I asked of him." I hadn't even heard her approaching.

I faced her, mouth slightly parted. I shook my head back and forth. "Why?"

She reached forward and grabbed my hand, placing mine in both of hers. "Follow me."

Donna released me and started walking away. Glancing back at Turner, he mouthed "sorry" to me, and followed his mom. This couldn't be happening. His family had officially lost their minds. What business could I possibly have here? I said my goodbyes the day my parents were placed into the ground. Did she want me to sit and talk to them? Sorry, but I wasn't one of those people. I didn't come here, lay on the grass and speak to them like they could hear me. If there was any place I felt my parents, it was at home. My arms were at my sides and I was feeling absolutely defeated. I didn't want to fight, and I didn't want to be here. Squaring my shoulders, I'd do whatever it is that she wanted me to do and then I would high tail it out of there. Donna wouldn't be hearing from me for a while. She had to know that this wasn't okay. In fact, I wasn't sure if I was going to be giving Turner the silent treatment after this as well. I knew one thing, when I got back home, I'd be asking him to leave. This was all just cruel.

Reluctantly, I walked behind them, keeping my distance. I went over every possible reason why I was brought here but nothing prepared me for seeing the rest of the Brooks clan. There they stood by a freshly dug plot and a small casket that was no bigger than the size of an . . . infant. I stopped in my tracks, my hand going to my mouth. I gasped, shaking my head back and forth. Turner heard me and started to come to my aid. Donna held him back and told him to go over with everyone else. When she approached me, she was very cautious.

"It's going to be okay," she told me.

My mouth opened and closed. "Is that?" I didn't want to finish.

She nodded. "I made a few phone calls. I know you probably don't want to be here or do this, but when this pain starts to feel a little less and you think about Noah, I want you to know exactly where he is, and that he had a place . . . with you."

Tears welled in my eyes. I was speechless. The anger I'd previously felt was pushed back and sadness seeped into me. "But the rest of the family is here."

She looked confused. "Of course they are. Don't you know why?"

I shook my head no.

A serene smile came across her lips. "Because, honey, my Turner has fallen for you. The moment I saw it, you became family, and that means we are *all* here for you."

"I don't understand."

"You will. Come." She guided me to where everyone was standing.

Turner took my hand and gave it a squeeze. Paul stood in front of everyone and spoke.

"Annabelle, I want you to know that we are all deeply sorry for your loss. You've been dealt some very challenging hands in your short life, and yet you seem to have handled it all with grace and dignity. Instead of making decisions to hide from what God has put on your plate, you showed perseverance during what could be the most trying time in a person's life." He paused and looked directly at me. "And now this. I know none of us may truly understand how you could be feeling at this very moment or for the last couple of days, but we wanted you to know one thing—you are family. You are part of something bigger than you think. Donna and myself, and of course our boys, we are here for you. Anything you may need, all you have to do is ask. Although we may get nosey and just assume we know what's best for you." They all let out a small chuckle. "I'm sure you can tell by what my wife has done here. This is not a traditional funeral or anything. Why Donna chose to do this was simply because Noah deserved a place to rest, and you, my dear, you deserved peace of mind and to know because you have a place with us, so did he."

I couldn't take it anymore. My tears turned into a river, and I was full on sobbing. Never in my life would I have thought people would care enough about me to do something like this. Paul wasn't done. Just as his last words left his mouth, he stepped aside. I was too preoccupied by the gathering of everyone, and the baby's casket, I hadn't even seen what had been behind him. There was a small grave stone that read:

Baby Noah
Oct 21, 2015
Loved by one, felt by many

I went to my knees. Turner had the mind to try and catch me, but I shooed him away. I needed my space. "Oh my God," I whispered. Both of my hands were covering my mouth and my cheeks were soaked. "I never even thought . . ." I trailed off. If a person was capable of sensory overload, I was having it. My brain didn't want to wrap around the possibility that there were such generous people in this world, or people who thought beyond themselves to do such a kind thing.

I glanced up at everyone around me as they all watched me. Turner, Donna, Paul, Wrigley, Dodger, Camden, and Keegan. Macie wasn't there, but it was okay. "Family," I said out loud. "This is what a family is."

Turner kneeled by me. "Yeah, beautiful, this is family." He kissed my forehead and wiped some of my tears away.

"Thank you," I whispered.

Keegan sniffled, and Camden put his arm around her.

"Anybody need a joke to lighten the mood?" Wrigley asked.

Dodger slapped the back of his head. I'm starting to think that was his defense against anything that made him uncomfortable—making people laugh.

"Geez, so dead around here," he grumbled.

"Wrig, go wait in the car, would ya?" Paul sighed.

A giggle bubbled up my throat. I couldn't help it. "He doesn't have to go. It's okay."

Reaching his hand out to me, Wrigley offered to help me up. Turner growled. I took it and stood.

"You're my girl, Belle."

"Thank you." I beamed. "In fact, thank you to all of you. Especially you, Donna. I don't know how you knew what to do, but you did. I've not been a part of a family in so long, that this is truly overwhelming. Noah was a very special boy. All I wanted for him in his short life was to know and feel what love was. I hope he did." A single tear streaked down my face.

"No doubt he did," Turner said, pulling me into an embrace.

"You're in trouble Mr.," I mumbled into his chest.

"Wouldn't expect anything less," he replied.

A groundskeeper approached all of us and asked if he could go ahead with lowering the casket into the ground. He said we could stay to watch if we wanted. I didn't. This was all more than I could handle in one day, and I felt like I was ready for a nap.

"Would you two like to come to the house for dinner? Won't take me long to whip something up," Donna offered. "In fact I'd like all of you to come, boys."

"Thanks, Mom. But I've gone some plans with Annabelle this afternoon."

My eyes shot to Turner's. "What now?"

"You'll see."

Great! He may not live to see another day the way he was going with all the unexpected stuff today.

"Oh, Donna?" I called her back before she had gone too far.

"Yes, dear?"

I looked at the ground and swallowed the lump in my throat. "Th-thanks. For this. For all of this. For Noah and me. It was more than I could have ever expected or known I wanted."

Her eyes became glassy. She strode toward me and pulled me into the most caring and motherly embrace I'd received since my own mom had held me.

"Always."

She turned and walked away. Family . . . it really was the cornerstone or foundation of who we are.

"Turner," I warned.

"Before you say anything, just hear me out."

"No. No, no, no. And I mean absolutely not!"

"Annabelle, you're getting worked up over nothing."

His "nothing" was certainly something. I was currently standing in front of a building that had a sign on the outside that said: *Touch the sky, and fall to the earth.*

What. The. Fuck.

"This isn't nothing, Turner Brooks. Did you actually think I was going to bungee jump?"

"No, but I thought maybe if I asked nicely enough, you might." He gave me puppy eyes. Which was a new one for him.

"There aren't enough words in the English language that would explain how crazy I think you are right now. Today of all days you want to do this?" He was certifiable.

"Listen." He stepped forward and grasped my face with both hands. "You know I have my reasons behind everything I do. I knew you were going to fight me on this one, but you need to hear me out."

My eyes darted back and forth between his. "I just watched a baby being buried today, I've been crying my eyes out for days, I have a headache, and now you want me to fling myself off a platform, attached to a cable and expect that it acts like a rubber band? Turner, this is way worse than some zip lining course."

"Kind of, but again, I have my reasons for asking you to do this. At least come to the top with me and see what it's like from up there."

Nerves were setting in. So was anger. "For fuck's sake, the view is probably just as I'm picturing. I don't need to go up there to see it."

He released me and started toward the lift. I called after him but he ignored me. Bastard knew I'd follow just to keep bitching at him. And I did exactly that the whole ride up. I had no clue what these things were called—we were on a platform similar to what we were on when we did the zip line. An electric lift raised us up as high as it would extend. It was really windy up there and I gripped the rails. I had a harness attaching me to the railing as a safety measure and the man who brought us up was giving us instruction for when we jumped. I heard nothing. My heart was in my throat and I wanted to puke. Could this headache get any worse?

"Annabelle?" Turner was standing there looking concerned.

"Huh?"

"Did you hear anything I just said?"

I was sweating so much, it was dripping down the side of my hair line. I shouldn't be sweating. It was cool outside, and being this high up it was even cooler.

"Were you talking?" I asked confused.

He brought his blue eyes down to my level. "Look at me. You've been through a lot. Today was not a good day, and there are a lot of things at play right now. But I needed you to know something."

"What's that?" I asked inquisitively.

"I'm here, Annabelle. I'm here and I'm not going anywhere. The past two or three months we've been getting to know each other I've come to the realization that I've been taking life for granted. Being a doctor, I've not noticed just how out of touch I have been, which is why I think I'm always looking for the next big thrill. You *are* my thrill, Annabelle. I look forward to seeing you every day. I love our crazy back and forth flirting. I love how you push my buttons and I make you step out of your comfort zone. But I love even more that you trust me enough that you do it."

As if I hadn't cried enough today. "Turner," I softly spoke his name.

"I know you think today isn't a good day to do something like this, but I think it's a perfect day. Want to know why?"

"Why?"

"Because you need to know that life keeps moving. The longer you sit back and watch as things happen around you, you're not living the one that you were given. I don't want to see you live in fear that something awful is going to happen. And every step you take . . . I'm right there with you. You jump off of this thing, I'm jumping too. Hell, we can go together and I'll hold you the whole way. You are no longer alone."

I sniffed. "Turner?"

He cleared his throat, knowing he'd just made the grandest speech of all speeches. "Yeah?"

I didn't want to think anymore, I just wanted to act. "I think I'm falling in love with you."

The sun was setting over some hills in the distance and the light was reflecting off of his vibrant blue eyes. He beamed even brighter than the sun and gave me a blinding smile. "Good, 'cause I think I'm falling too."

I was taken aback. I wasn't expecting him to reciprocate. Not at all. I simply wanted him to know where my feelings stood. Warmth was taking over my body, and I stepped into the protection of his body.

"We hooked up to this thing?" I asked over my shoulder.

The guy who had ridden up with us gave me a thumbs up. I don't think he wanted to intrude on our moment.

"What are you doing?" Turner asked.

"Take the leap, Turner."

"Right now?" he said surprised.

"Now. Don't make me say it twice."

"Yes, ma'am."

Without hesitation, he put his massive arms around me, asked the guy if we could go like together and next thing I knew, we were free falling. I had no idea how long we fell for. Seemed like minutes to me, but it was only seconds. We jerked hard when we reached the end of the line, and flew back up a little over halfway of the distance that we'd fallen. We bounced back and forth and swung like a pendulum several times. This was nothing like race car driving, or zip lining, or driving a Jeep, or, hell, even sex. Bungee jumping was straight up insane.

But falling in love was an absolute leap of faith. There was no comparison. I'd found something in this man that was communicating to my cold and closed off heart, and he was busting down those walls faster than I could keep putting them back up. He wasn't going to let me win this battle. Not now, and maybe not ever. And you know what? I was okay with that.

I hadn't made a single sound the whole time we were flying through the air, but as the machine lowered us to the ground I started laughing. I laughed hysterically. No doubt Turner thought I'd gone mad.

"What's so funny?" he asked, an amused expression on his face.

I shook my head, laughing even harder because we were hanging upside down and we both looked ridiculous. "Oh, just all of this. Today should have been the second worst day of my life, and somehow you made it okay. You showed me

I'm a part of a family again, and now you're teaching me how to live. Where did you come from, Doctor Brooks?"

He smirked. I knew a smart ass answer was on the tip of his tongue. "From snips and snails, and puppy dogs tails. And of course good genetics."

I chortled. "Always arrogant."

"Wouldn't be me if I wasn't."

"Hmmm, yes, I know."

When we were set on the ground, we both stood on our feet and regained our balance. I used his chest as a place to steady myself.

"Can we do this again sometime?"

I don't think he could be any more shocked than he was right now. "I suppose, if you really want too."

I nodded. "I do. But on one condition."

"And what's that?"

I reached up on my tippy toes and kissed his soft lips. "That you fall with me."

He smoothed my hair back and placed a kiss on my nose. "Always, Annabelle. Always."

With that I knew I was okay. I had loved, lost, and been loved. I was a part of something huge, and my life wouldn't be wasted sticking to the sidewalks. Turner Brooks was my future, and I planned on living it to the fullest as long as was by my side. I had a feeling that was going to be for a very long time to come.

THE END

EPILOGUE

Annabelle

"ANNABELLE, I THINK YOU HAVE a visitor," Keegan said from beside me. She nudged me with her elbow.

I looked up to where she was staring. Turner was walking towards me wearing his obnoxious white doctor's coat and a smile. I smirked. What was he up too?

As he approached me, his face turned serious. "Nurse Annabelle, I have some things I need to talk to you about."

I stood and straightened my scrubs. "Doctor Brooks. Does this pertain to a patient?"

"Actually, it has to do with your behavior and some complaints that I've received."

I jerked my head back. "Whomever had complaints hasn't come to me to discuss them, so as far as I'm concerned, I don't care."

"That's not the best attitude to have, Annabelle."

Keegan snorted. I glanced down at her and tapped her with my foot. "Oh sorry, I think I have a patient to check on. Have fun you two."

She took off down the hall. I brought my attention back to Turner. "Well, my attitude is none of your concern, Doctor. If there are any more complaints the HR department can come talk to me."

He frowned. Darting his bright blue eyes around, he took a step into me. "I think we should discuss this in private."

A snarky grunt came from across the counter. Little Miss Red Silk's lip was curled in disgust. I broke character for a brief moment and winked at her. Eat shit, honey, he's mine. I had the gratification that one of the many women Turner had once dated wasn't who he was searching for—he was looking for me. My gesture wasn't well received. Instead of watching the rest of our exchange, Robin stormed off down the hall. Served her right.

Turner cleared his throat. "Now that that's taken care of, what were we talking about?"

He broke character as well appearing amused.

"About that private talk . . ." I leaned into him and kissed his cheek.

Turner raised his brow. "I do believe that goes against protocol, Annabelle."

I stood on my tippy toes and nibbled on his ear, not caring who saw my public display of affection. "Protocol, schmotocol."

"What am I going to do with you?" I heard the smile in his voice.

"Whatever you want."

"Hmmm . . ." he whispered in my ear. "Find an empty room, *now*."

Who was I to argue? Twisting around, I began the short walk to the end of the hall where I knew a room was empty and we'd have a few moments alone. Turner swatted me on the butt, reminding me who was in charge. I shook my head and bit my lip. Only two months had gone by since Noah had passed, but I'd never been so happy. Yeah, Turner Brooks made me happy. He was life. He breathed it into me, and showed me who I could be. I learned how to smile again. I was my reason, but he was the teacher. For that I'd be forever grateful. I loved him and today, that's what mattered the most.

"In here, Doctor," I summoned, entering a room.

His eyes shifted from entertained to lustful. Oh yes, Turner Brooks was undoubtedly mine and I was going to keep him for as long as he'd have me.

—◇—◇—◇—

Macie

My hands shook furiously as I ripped open the box and pulled out the white sheet of paper. I laid it flat on the counter so I could read the instructions. My eyes scanned over the words.

"Ack, not fucking Spanish. Where's the English version?"

I searched vehemently for anything that said "Step one" or for an image to follow. It's not like I didn't know how to use these things. They played commercials all damn day for the women who stayed at home and watched soap operas. I've seen a few of them. But I wanted to make sure I was following the instructions to the letter. Any skipped stepped or timing or whatever could make it all invalid or false.

"Ha!" I said to myself.

I found it. It said to take the applicator out of the plastic wrap and place it in the urine stream for five seconds, then lay it flat. It would take two minutes for results to appear in the window. I sat on the toilet and tore the test open with my teeth. There was a purple cap on the end that I took off and tossed to the side. Thank God I needed to pee. I did exactly as it all said. Standing up, I pulled up my pants and hovered over the test, refusing to take my eyes off of it.

My finger nails tapped on the counter like I was playing Chopsticks on the piano. A nervous habit I had picked up since I was a kid.

Two minutes. Two fucking minutes.

Why did it take two minutes? This shit should show up right away. The idiots who created these things clearly didn't realize how time sensitive it was to know the answer right away. And honestly, why don't I wear a watch? Where in the hell did I put my cell phone? I should be timing this. I glanced around. It was nowhere near. Apparently, it was still in my purse on the bed.

"Damn," I grumbled under my breath.

My eyes went back to the little game changer on the counter. Something started to show up in the first box. What does that mean? Fuck, I didn't even finish reading all the instructions. I don't even know what I'm looking at. I searched. Okay, two lines is positive, one line is negative.

Two lines is positive . . . two lines is pos—oh God!

I was going to be sick. Rushing to the toilet, I flipped the lid and threw up. My stomach heaved so hard it hurt. Every ounce of food and coffee I'd inhaled this morning was now a mess of bile and disgustingness. I slid down 'til I was on my ass on the cold travertine tile of my bathroom. Tears streamed down my face and confusion wracked my brain. How did this happen? I was on birth control. It didn't make any sense. Was I part of that small two percent population that the pill wasn't effective for? God, I was going to sue the shit out of the company. Nobody was in the two percent. The two percent was just there to scare the shit out of people to take their pills on time. I was someone that took it at the same time every day.

What was I going to do? I looked up at the counter and saw the stick still sitting there. With uneasy fingers, I took hold of it and checked it again. I shook my head. The results hadn't changed. This wasn't supposed to happen.

I was pregnant, and it was Dodger's. My life was about to be flipped upside down.

ACKNOWLEDGEMENTS

To my family, especially my kids, thank you for being the faces that push me forward every day. Picking up my slack when there was too much going on, and for always being understanding. I love you all very much.

Missy, I have no clue how you deal with my wishy washy ass, but you do and you take it in stride. Pushing back deadlines, understanding why I took long pauses, and then taking the time to tell me to pull up my big girl panties and get my shit done. You've known the right words to tell me when I needed to hear them. A good editor is invaluable, I hope I begged enough to keep you around. Please keep tolerating me!

To my group of beta readers: Beth, Stacey, Heather, Shelly, Diane and Nichole. You women are amazing. You all read the book in record time, in a crunch, and provided me some incredible feedback and suggestions. I'm so grateful to each of you and that you took a chance on me.

Nichole, you've become the best friend I didn't know I was looking for. Every single day, you deal with my crazy. And we both know it's crazy. I don't know why you stick around, but you do. I've come to rely on you for so much and I adore you. Thank you for being you, and not giving up on me.

Made in the USA
Middletown, DE
07 September 2018